A Candlelight Ecstasy Romance ™

"LET ME LOVE YOU, SARA. LET ME SHOW YOU HOW I FEEL."

Sara slid her arms around his waist, lured by his words. Roarke pulled her still more tightly against him. Bringing his face close to hers, he placed soft, lingering kisses on her cheeks, and Sara could feel her face grow warm wherever his lips touched her skin. Then his mouth tenderly sought hers. His kiss was gentle at first but soon grew demanding. Clinging to him in a passionate embrace, Sara was surprised to find herself responding with equal fervor.

INTIMATE
STRANGERS

Denise Mathews

A CANDLELIGHT ECSTASY ROMANCE ™

Published by
Dell Publishing Co., Inc.
1 Dag Hammarskjold Plaza
New York, New York 10017

Dell ® TM 681510, Dell Publishing Co., Inc.
Candlelight Ecstasy Romance™ is a trademark of
Dell Publishing Co., Inc., New York, New York.

ISBN: 0-440-14048-X

Printed in the United States of America
First printing—January 1983

To Our Readers:

We have been delighted with your enthusiastic response to Candlelight Ecstasy Romances™, and we thank you for the interest you have shown in this exciting series.

In the upcoming months we will continue to present the distinctive sensuous love stories you have come to expect only from Ecstasy. We look forward to bringing you many more books from your favorite authors and also the very finest work from new authors of contemporary romantic fiction.

As always, we are striving to present the unique, absorbing love stories that you enjoy most—books that are more than ordinary romance.

Your suggestions and comments are always welcome. Please write to us at the address below.

Sincerely,

The Editors
Candlelight Romances
1 Dag Hammarskjold Plaza
New York, New York 10017

INTIMATE
STRANGERS

CHAPTER ONE

A brilliant, hot white glare made the pain in her head increase to an unbearable degree. The throbbing became an agony of exquisite proportions and she groaned, closing her eyes tightly against the luminous torture. A wave of alarm swelled through her body, followed by the sensation of overwhelming terror. She heard that same sound again and was dimly aware it was coming from her. She was moaning, moaning from pain, a pain that was everywhere, like the dazzling, searing radiance that had blinded her.

A disembodied voice floated through the fog of pain that clouded her brain. "Can you hear me? I thought I saw you open your eyes a moment ago. Can you answer me?"

She struggled to break through the layers of mist that gripped her mind. She felt as though she were deep in a bottomless sea and labored to penetrate the viscous misery that engulfed her body.

Tentatively squinting, she barely opened her eyes and tried to make them focus but was fearful that the same brilliance would assault her again. There were rows of lights in the ceiling over her head and the walls were stark white. Slowly she turned her head and blinked her eyes to clear her vision and realized someone was standing beside her, and behind that someone were a number of forbidding machines positioned along the side of the room. "Where am I? Am I all right?" To her surprise, her voice was barely a husky whisper. But the dark-haired woman, dressed in white, watching her, had heard the murmured questions.

The woman's face was expressionless except for her eyes, which seemed to be warm and kind. "Well, hello, you're back with us at last! You're in the hospital, but you're going to be fine." She patted her on the hand reassuringly.

Trying to grasp the woman's hand, her own flailed aimlessly about in the air. It felt so weak and, with dismay, she watched her arm drop limply back onto the bed. "Hos-hospital? How did I get here?" Her throat felt raw and her voice sounded hoarse, but she persisted. "I can't move. What happened to me? Please, I'm scared, I hurt everywhere." She tried to move her arm again to grasp at the woman and this time succeeded in taking hold of the woman's forearm.

The nurse gently took her hand away and said soothingly, "Now, try to calm down. You've been in an accident, but you're going to be all right. I'm going to call your doctor and tell him you're awake. He'll answer your questions."

She watched the nurse move over to the phone that hung on the wall opposite her bed. After a low, mumbled conversation, the crisp white figure came back to the bed, smiling as she picked up her limp arm and wrapped a black cuff around it. Her brain spun, full of half-formed questions as the nurse took her blood pressure and pulse. Finally she couldn't keep silent any longer, but when she opened her mouth to speak, the nurse put a thermometer into it. She tried to quell the panic that was threatening to overwhelm her. What happened? What kind of accident had she had? She felt as though her body had been battered by something or someone, and her head ached horribly. *Oh, why won't someone explain why I feel like this,* she groaned inwardly.

As the nurse was writing some notes on a chart, a tall man in a white coat walked soundlessly into the room. "Good evening, young lady, I'm Dr. Maxwell." The doctor's smile lit up his eyes.

"What am I doing here?" She struggled to sit up but fell back on the bed, swamped by the aches and pains that wracked her body when she moved. Her chest felt constricted and the pain in her head made her senses swim.

"Wait, I'll raise your bed a little. We'll talk for a few minutes if you feel up to it, and I'll try to answer any questions you have. But you must promise me you'll try to stay calm." She watched as he raised the bed and moved the chair the nurse had vacated closer to the side of the bed where she could see him without moving her head around.

Her throat felt raspy and dry and she swallowed tightly, hoping to relieve the feeling. "Why am I in a hospital and what's wrong with me?" she whispered.

"Do you remember driving in a bad ice storm?" The doctor's voice was gentle and soothing.

Her brow wrinkled with concentration. "Ice storm? No, I . . ." An icy shiver of fear ran up her spine. "I don't remember any ice storm, I don't remember anything." Her voice choked off a sob. "What's wrong with me?" she wailed, and large tears rolled down her sensitive cheeks.

The doctor watched her reactions intently. Her fingers plucked nervously at the sheets that covered her bruised body and he saw the effort to concentrate was draining her quickly. Reaching out, the doctor took her hand and held it gently, trying to transfer some warmth and reassurance from his hand to hers. "There was an unexpected ice storm; you were driving your car and a small truck slid into you. You were lucky that neither one of you was going very fast. But you suffered a concussion, two broken ribs, and a broken ankle. One of your ribs punctured your lung and I had to operate to repair the damage. This is why you feel so much pain right now. You've had a rough time for a couple of days and you've been unconscious for most of it." He paused as he saw she was becoming agitated again and he didn't want to upset her any more than was necessary. "Now, come on, calm down, you're going to be fine. You'll have to stay in the hospital for a while, but in a couple of months, this will all seem like a bad dream." He smiled encouragingly at her and patted

11

her shoulder, hoping he had convinced her that she would be all right.

She dropped her head back down on the pillow. "Why can't I remember any of this? A storm? A car accident? How could anyone forget these things? I'm telling you, I don't remember! There's something horribly wrong." Her voice rose hysterically and her eyes darted around the room seeking escape from the pain and fear that trapped her. "Don't you understand what I'm saying? I can't even remember who I am! I can't remember my own name! You're lying to me, I know you're not telling me everything . . . I . . ."

"No, no. I'm not lying to you. I promise you that I've told you the truth and that you're going to be all right." The doctor interrupted with an earnestness that stopped her frenzied outburst. "You have a severe concussion and loss of memory is not at all uncommon. As you start to get better and your bruised brain heals, I feel sure this lapse of memory will disappear. What you need right now is rest and quiet and I'm going to make sure that you get it." Dr. Maxwell stood up and started to push the chair away from the bed.

Frantically she reached out and grasped the edge of his white coat and looked at him pleadingly. "Could you at least tell me my name? Tell me who I am . . . please!"

Again the doctor took hold of her hand, gently forcing her to release her grip on his lab coat and held her trembling fingers in his warm clasp. "Of course I can tell you your name. It's Sara . . . Sara Alexander."

A nurse appeared in the doorway. "Dr. Maxwell, you have a phone call."

The doctor glanced over his shoulder at her. "I'll be right there." Turning back to Sara, he said, "I have to leave, but I'll be back to see you tomorrow morning. We'll talk again and I'll try to answer any other questions you have. But, for now, I want you to rest. You're going to be fine." He smiled reassuringly.

When he tried to release her hand, she held on to him with

desperation. "Don't leave me, I don't have anyone, please don't leave me," she begged.

The doctor eased himself back into the chair and brushed the hair off her forehead with a caressing motion. "Sara, don't be so frightened; you're not alone," he murmured soothingly. "I'll be here to help you any way I can. But there's someone else who can help you far better than I." He stroked her forehead again. "You're married and your husband's been here at the hospital almost from the moment they brought you to the emergency room."

Sara's eyes opened wide in disbelief. "My husband! I'm married?"

"Yes, you are and I must say that's quite a man you have there. He'll be so relieved to hear you're conscious. Now, no more questions. You need to sleep, so I'm going to have the nurse give you a shot and the next time you wake up, you'll feel a little better and all this won't seem quite so frightening." The doctor smiled warmly, mumbled something to the nurse, and left the room before Sara could ask him anything else.

Sara closed her eyes. *What in the world is wrong with me?* she moaned to herself. *How could anyone forget everything?* Sara's brow furrowed and a deep pain slashed across her forehead, making white sparks dance behind her closed eyes. *Sara Alexander . . . Sara Alexander,* she repeated to herself, but her mind remained a pain-wracked blank. No images, no faces, no memories. Then the sound of the doctor's words filled the void. "You're married and your husband's been here at the hospital. . . ." *Married! Husband!* Her mind rebelled at the words. *How can I be married and not remember that? And whom am I married to? What does he look like?* She pressed her eyelids together in concentration as she tried to recall what he looked like, tried to remember his face. *Face!* Of course, her face! *Surely you couldn't forget your own face. I know if I looked into a mirror and saw my face, I'd remember everything.* She raised her head slowly and saw the nurse standing at the foot of the bed checking a hypodermic needle filled with a colorless fluid. "Nurse, could I please have a mirror?" she asked weakly.

"Not now, Mrs. Alexander. I'm going to give you a shot so you can go to sleep. When you wake up, I'll check with Dr. Maxwell about giving you a mirror." The nurse lowered the needle and injected it into her arm without further conversation. Soon Sara's eyes were heavy and she drifted off to sleep, a sleep where there was no mystery or pain.

Opening her eyes abruptly, Sara was released from the nightmare that had been gripping her. She was still groggy and the nightmarish feeling clung to the edges of her mind. The man in her dream seemed familiar to her, but she couldn't connect a name with the face. The harder she tried to get his face into focus, the more it dissipated, and the man's face that had been so clear when she was asleep was now just a fuzzy remnant. Somehow, though, she knew, that in some way, he was very important to her.

"Good morning, Mrs. Alexander."

Sara turned her head and saw a nurse standing beside her bed. She had been so intent on recalling the man's face that had appeared in her nightmare, her mind hadn't registered another presence in the room.

The nurse was hovering over the bed, fussing with her pillows and straightening the sheets. "It's a beautiful morning. We're supposed to have temperatures in the middle sixties today. I hope that means winter is over and spring is here to stay." The nurse prattled on as she lifted Sara's arm to take her pulse. "Washington, D.C., is at its most beautiful in the spring, although the cherry blossoms are going to be late blooming this year, but I love living here."

Some of the nurse's banal chatter penetrated Sara's mind. *Spring! I don't even remember winter!* She felt so bewildered and frightened and her thoughts whirled around in her head. *Isn't there anything I can remember?* Sara put her free hand up to rub

14

her aching head. "Excuse me, what did you say?" asked Sara, realizing the nurse was speaking to her again.

"I said, your head will still ache a bit, but it's nothing to worry about. It's just the last dregs of the concussion you have. I'm going to give you a sponge bath then your breakfast because Dr. Maxwell will be coming in soon to check you and I'd like you to be ready for his examination." The nurse moved to the foot of Sara's bed and wrote some notes on a chart.

"Yes, that's fine, anything you wish," Sara mumbled distractedly. Dr. Maxwell . . . she vaguely remembered him. He was that big burly man with unruly salt-and-pepper hair who had been so comforting to her last night . . . or was it last night? She wasn't sure of anything anymore. People had come and gone, floating through her semiconsciousness and between the pain and the drugged stupor she was kept in; people and time meant nothing.

She tried to focus her mind on Dr. Maxwell. He was the man who had tried to explain to her why she was in a hospital. He had told her she had amnesia from a concussion, that she had been in a car accident. She felt almost triumphant! She could remember him and what he had told her. So why would he say she had amnesia? She could faintly recall them moving her from Intensive Care to this room. But the memory was more like a dream, and she suddenly realized she couldn't remember anything that had happened before that.

Once again her mind churned and caused that now familiar sense of befogging pain. A ball of quivering anxiety shot through her chest to meet and increase the ache in her head. She was married! He had told her that she was married! How could she forget such a thing? The idea that she couldn't remember her husband frightened her and made her feel disoriented.

She had to concentrate on something she knew she remembered; maybe that would break the grip of this immobilizing fear. Testing herself, she tried to remember Dr. Maxwell's face in greater detail. It was craggy with graying eyebrows. Of course, her face! "Nurse, could I please have a mirror?" Sara tried to sit up but grabbed her side and winced with pain.

The nurse came over to the side of her bed and gently settled her back onto the pillow. "Mrs. Alexander, you must keep in mind that you have had surgery. We encourage our patients to move about and sit up, but please do it slowly. These quick moves and thrashing around could hurt you. Now, I'll raise your bed and you can fill out your menu for tomorrow. And after I've given you a sponge bath, I'll bring in your breakfast."

With quick efficiency the nurse clutched the control and along with a low, humming noise, Sara felt the bed move and soon found herself in a sitting position. A tray table was placed across her bed, a menu and a pencil on the tray, and the nurse was out of her room before Sara could ask her again about having a mirror. Frustration brought quick tears to her eyes and her thoughts raced through her brain so rapidly, they almost tumbled over each other. *There's something wrong that they don't want me to see. It must be my face! What's wrong with my face that no one will give me a mirror?*

With trembling fingertips she tentatively touched her cheeks and flinched from the slight touch. The flesh was tender and sore, but she felt no bandages until her exploring fingers reached her forehead where there was a small square of gauze. Other than the small patch and the soreness, there didn't seem to be any cuts or stitches. She traced the moisture from her tears down her cheeks and shuddered, knowing that she had to try to keep some control over her emotions. What she wanted to do was to scream with outrage that she was thrust into this alien existence. But she knew if she let go and caved in to her fear, she would give up any chance to rebuild her life. She knew that weakness and tears wouldn't solve the situation nor heal her wounds.

Sara wiped the tears from her eyes and with determination took the pencil in her hand and quickly filled out the menu. She sighed and laid her head back against the pillow. Suddenly a light of hope flickered in her mind and she felt a surge of joy.

She picked up the menu and looked at it in wonder. Grasping the pencil in her right hand, she sensed how comfortable it felt there. Again tears came to her eyes but now for a different reason. She liked sugar and milk in her coffee and held a pencil in her right hand! Excitedly she kissed the menu and waved the pencil in the air. At least she knew these things instinctively and if she could remember this, there must be hope for remembering everything else.

She lay in her bed propped up by several pillows, waiting for the doctor to come to her room. She felt a little better, in fact had almost enjoyed eating the soft-boiled egg and cereal she had been served for breakfast. The nurse had sponge-bathed her and had brushed her hair back and caught it with a clip at the nape. Thinking was not quite so painful, and her thoughts were a little clearer. She supposed it was from the realization she could remember something and that had given her hope. But she had to have some answers if she was going to be able to cope, and the most important answer she needed was to the question of how long this amnesia would last. Deep in thought, she was barely aware when the doctor breezed into the room.

"Good morning, Mrs. Alexander." He took a chart from the waiting nurse and studied it. After a quick conference with the nurse, he walked over and stood beside Sara's bed. As he examined her, he said, "I see you've been a model patient—slept all night and ate a good breakfast. How do you feel today?" He finished probing her and pulled the chair close beside her bed and sat down.

"Except for a sore head, sore side, a lead foot, and a numb brain, I guess I'm okay. But why won't anyone give me a mirror? Is there something wrong with my face?" Sara demanded.

"You are indeed feeling better, Sara. May I call you Sara?" he asked with a pleased look on his face, amused by her bravado.

The smile that quivered around her mouth made the skin on her face tingle with twinges of pain. "You can call me Joe and I wouldn't know whether you were talking to me or not!" The laughter in her eyes was slowly replaced by a haunted expression. "Why won't anyone give me a mirror?" she asked in a small shaky voice.

Dr. Maxwell took her hand and squeezed it. "Because I told them not to give you one. Your face is bruised and swollen and you have a bandage on your forehead. Even if you could remember everything, you wouldn't recognize yourself. I'll strike a bargain with you. As soon as the swelling goes down and the bruises start to fade, I'll hand you a mirror myself." He smiled at her and thought to himself that he could see her beauty beneath the bruises and that she must really be a lovely woman. He squeezed her hand again.

"It's a deal," Sara replied, in control of herself once more. "How long will it be before I can remember anything about me?"

The doctor shook his head. "I don't know how long the amnesia will last. It's a very peculiar occurrence, but I think once you're back home and in familiar surroundings, things will come back to you a lot more quickly. I wish I could tell you more, but to be perfectly truthful, I really don't know. Your head will hurt for a few more days because of the very severe concussion, but the confusion you feel is probably more from the anesthetic and pain killers than the bump on your head. You must take things slowly and not push yourself. Try to take it day by day, although I know it's hard to do. If you remember something, fine, just don't try to reach for it. Let the memories come to you."

Sara nodded her head in exasperated agreement. "I found that out this morning when I woke up from a nightmare. The harder I tried to recall a face I had seen in my dream, the more quickly the face faded. But I'm desperate; I have to remember." Sara turned her head away with such a forlorn look on her face that Dr. Maxwell gasped. "Sara, don't try so hard, it will come."

He held her hand lightly. "Your husband would like to see you for a few minutes. Do you feel up to that?"

"I don't know . . ." Sara looked up at him, hoping he would give her the answer.

18

"I don't think it would be such a bad idea for you to see him. I feel sure he can answer your questions better than I. The poor guy's been here five days now, waiting to see you awake. Every time he's been in to see you, you've been unconscious or sound asleep. I've told him not to stay too long this visit because you still need plenty of rest and no excitement. Remember what I said though, don't reach for the answers, let them come to you. Frustration isn't going to help you at all. I'll be in to see you again this evening." He walked to the door then turned to look at her with an impish grin on his face. "Take care of yourself . . . Joe!"

Sara laughed weakly as he swept out the door, his white coat flapping around his knees. Dr. Maxwell's sense of humor and his genuine concern made her feel almost confident that she would get well and remember everything.

A nurse appeared in the doorway as Dr. Maxwell left. "Would you like me to ask your husband to come in now?"

"Yes, please." Sara wiped her palms nervously on the sheet and took a deep breath, fear mixing with hope. Maybe when she saw him, the past would all come back to her but . . . but what if it didn't . . . ?

Following the nurse, a tall, well-built man came into the room, carrying a huge bouquet of flowers in his arms. Sara's breath caught in her throat; she knew she had seen his face before, but where? Then the veil of forgetfulness shifted just a little. His face . . . it was the face of the man in her nightmare. That's the only way his face was familiar to her. Not a flicker of recognition, of memory, or anything else. Just that he was the man from her dream!

CHAPTER TWO

The extremely handsome man stood in the doorway observing Sara stare at him. She lowered her eyes and looked down at her hands held tightly clenched in her lap. Again Sara felt disoriented. It was as though she was thrust back into the middle of her nightmare. *Am I awake or asleep? Is this some trick my mind is playing on me? This is my husband? Is he real?* She glanced back up at him and met the cobalt blue eyes that unwaveringly watched her.

Then a slight smile lifted the corners of his full lips. "From the expression on your face, anyone would think you just saw a ghost." His deep voice had a rich warm timbre that resonated around the room. The smile on his lips crinkled his eyes at the corners. Looking around for a place to put the flowers, he handed them to the nurse who took them and left the room. "Have I changed that much, Sara?"

Sara wanted to cry out to the nurse not to leave her alone with this—this man she didn't know, but by the time she opened her mouth to call her back, the white figure disappeared. She watched as the dark-haired man walked over to her, and when she saw his arms reach out to her, she flinched and tried to bury herself deeper into the pillows. But his arms slid around her and she felt herself gently but firmly being nestled against his body. The aroma of his cologne and the faint smell of tobacco made the strangest sense of peace come over her. She sighed deeply and for a moment leaned her head against his chest.

"You didn't answer my question, Sara. Why did you look at me so strangely?" he murmured in her hair as he kissed the top of her head.

Even though his voice was no more than a husky whisper, she could feel its vibrating on her cheek. She stiffened and pulled away from him. "I don't know how to answer your question. I . . . I . . . don't know you, so how would I know if you've changed? Seeing you in the doorway startled me because I . . . I think I dreamed about you last night."

The stranger took her face between his hands and looked at her with the tenderest expression. "Dr. Maxwell told me you have amnesia, but I find it hard to believe. Don't you really know me? Sara, don't you remember anything at all? How could you dream about me if you don't remember me?"

Sara put her hands over his and pulled them away from her face. "Please, don't, I'm so confused. I don't know why I dreamed about you because I don't know you," she repeated emphatically.

The imposing figure straightened up and he stood with his fists on his hips, never moving his eyes from her face. Sara wanted to scream at him to quit staring as if she were some side-show freak. Much to her relief, he sat down in the chair beside the bed, but his examination of her face still made her feel like a specimen under a microscope. His eyes narrowed just the slightest bit as he scrutinized her. Then he reached out and took her hand in his. She felt like she was touching something searing hot. Her fingers recoiled, but his grasp tightened and imprisoned her very cold hand.

"Sara, thank God you're going to be all right. When I think of what could have happened . . ." His lids closed down over the piercing blue irises and a small shudder ran through his body.

Sara impulsively tightened her hand; for some reason a feeling of compassion rose in her for this man. "I'm sorry, I don't mean to be such a worry to you. It's just so confusing. In fact, it's frightening not to be able to remember anything. There are so many things . . . I didn't even know my own name until Dr. Maxwell told me." Her eyes filled with tears and she became angry with herself. She just wouldn't break down and cry right now. If she let her self-pity overcome her, he would begin to pity her and she didn't want this man's pity. She wanted his help.

"I'm sorry. I guess I'm weaker than I thought." Sara turned her head away then looked back at him. "Am I really married to you?" she asked pleadingly.

"Stop apologizing, I feel sure you'll remember everything soon." He dropped her hand, stood up, and walked to the foot of the bed.

Sara saw the opaque curtain drop over his clear eyes. He had rebuffed her and she felt embarrassed. *How can I get my memory back if I don't have his help?* she thought dejectedly. She felt her embarrassment growing. *I can't ask this man any questions, even if he is my husband, if he shuts me off like this.* She searched desperately for the right thing to say, but the silence between them grew. The phone rang and Sara, startled out of her black thoughts, tried to reach it but gasped, grabbed her side, and fell back on the bed.

"I'll answer it," the pacing man said tersely. After a few words into the black receiver, he turned to Sara. "It's my office, do you mind?"

Shaking her head, Sara studied the man who was concentrating on what was being said to him over the telephone. He was a tall man and powerfully built. The dark suit fit snugly across his broad shoulders and followed his body smoothly, tapering at his narrow waist and hips. His hair was dark and wavy with just a dusting of silver at the temples. His large hands and graceful long narrow fingers gripped the phone receiver, and his handsome face with its straight nose and strong jaw was taut with intense attention that made the sensuousness of his mouth harden into a straight line. But the most arresting thing about him were his eyes. They were a warm, vibrant blue and his dark tan made them appear even more startling. Her emotions were in a turmoil. How could she forget such a man? How could anyone forget a man who looks like he does? Why didn't his face evoke any memories?

He hung up the receiver and came over beside her again. "Do you need anything? Would you like me to bring in some of your own nightgowns?"

Sara stared at him mutely. A picture had suddenly flashed in her mind. She saw two people in a bedroom. The man was sitting up in a bed, his bare, hairy chest exposed above the light-colored sheet. His head was thrown back against the pillow and he was laughing at a girl who was standing beside the bed wearing the silliest pajamas. "Darling, where on earth did you get that thing? No one over five would wear pajamas like those." The girl was pretending to be insulted. "I thought you'd love them. You complain about my cold feet all the time." The girl beside the bed was pirouetting so the man could see the full effect of her outfit. The pajamas were onepiece with a zipper up the front and bootielike feet. The man was still laughing as he reached up and drew the girl down onto the bed. Slowly he pulled the zipper down and, as he nuzzled her neck, he whispered, "It's not your cold feet that really bother me . . . it's you that bothers me!"

The picture faded and Sara realized the man standing beside her was staring down at her, puzzlement clouding his face.

"Are you all right? Do you want me to get the nurse?" He took her hand in his and a warmth flooded through her body.

She felt confused both by the flash of memory and her reaction to his touch. "No, I don't need a nurse, I'm fine."

A concerned frown flickered across his brow. "Then what's wrong, Sara?"

She grasped his hand tightly. "I've just had the strangest thing happen. When you asked me if I wanted my own nightgown, my mind was suddenly filled with a picture of you lying in bed laughing at a young girl who was showing off some ridiculous pajamas with feet." Sara glanced up at his face to see his eyes dancing with the memory.

23

"Oh, yes, that awful red flannel outfit!" He laughed and kissed the back of her hand. The touch of his lips flustered her. "The girl was you, Sara, when we were first married. When you came out of the bathroom that night in those outrageous pajamas, I just about fell out of bed laughing. You looked so cute . . . silly, but cute." He smiled at her lovingly.

Sara tore her eyes away from his. This man loved her and she couldn't remember him except in connection with some stupid pajamas. She felt guilty, then sorrow surfaced through the guilt. She knew she had lost more than her memories; she had lost their sense of intimacy.

"Don't look so sad, Sara, we'll work this out together, I promise," he murmured fervently, his voice husky. He bent down and kissed her on the temple, his lips lingering on her brow. "I have to leave now, but I'll be back this evening with some of your things," he assured her. "If you should need anything before then, call me at this number." He handed her a small card on which a telephone number was written. "I'll see you this evening, my love." His eyes moved over her face. His brow was slightly creased and there was a poignancy to his expression as he lightly touched her bruised cheek.

Sara winced inwardly and closed her eyes. His tender gesture expressed his love and sympathy for her more clearly than words. *How must I look to this man, my husband?* Tentatively she raised her hand to her cheek. *If only they would give me a mirror.*

Sensing his withdrawal, she opened her eyes and realized he was near the door, ready to leave. Calling out to him, she said in a small wispy voice, "Please, forgive me . . ." she hesitated.

"Forgive you for what?" he asked gently.

Her eyes found his and as she gazed deeply into the blue depths, she found the courage she was seeking. "Would you tell me your . . . your . . ." she stammered, "your first name?" She broke their eye contact and lowered her lids; she didn't want him to see her embarrassment.

24

"It's Roarke, Sara," he stated simply and quietly opened the door. He turned back to her and said, "Darling, please don't be embarrassed; we'll work this out. I'll help you any way I can; I just want you well again." Roarke walked through the doorway and out of Sara's line of vision, just as he had in her dream.

Turning to look out the window, Sara's thoughts drifted back over the long, lonely, fearful days she had spent in this nightmare. She was feeling better; she knew her physical health and strength were improving daily. Smiling to herself, she remembered the first time the nurse had helped her to get to her feet and taught her how to use crutches. It had been miserably funny. Her side pulled and twinged as she learned to hobble around her room and she'd fall into the chair by the window exhausted from her attempts to become mobile.

Then frustration and fear mixed with a little sadness welled up in her throat. *Damn,* she thought, pressing her forehead to the back of the armchair, *when am I going to get well mentally? When will my memory come back? When mental images do flash through my mind, they fade away too fast for me to hold on to them.*

Dr. Maxwell's and Roarke's visits were the bright spots in her days although Roarke's emotional swings mystified and sometimes terrified her. He could be so charming and loving one minute that she would almost wallow in gratitude. Then that dark curtain would fall over his eyes, especially when she asked anything about their past. It was as if he didn't want her to remember, and her feeling that he had spurned her and her attempts to get answers rankled her. If he did answer her questions, it was with terse replies. It was as if he were building a wall between them. *But on the other hand,* Sara thought, *I really can't blame him. It must hurt him that I can't remember our life together.*

Most of her half-formed feelings about Roarke were of sadness and regret. Sara had thought several times that maybe they had

had an argument before her accident, but she hesitated to ask him. She didn't know if she wanted to hear that answer right now or could cope with what she might hear.

But today was going to be something special and maybe a day that would see an end to this mystery that engulfed her. Dr. Maxwell had promised her that today she could have a mirror. Impatiently she waited for the doctor to arrive; her anticipation and apprehension were becoming unbearable. Would she recognize the face reflected in the glass? What did she look like? What color were her eyes? She wanted to get out of the chair and run away from the possibility that the face in the mirror would be the face of a stranger. But where would she go?

"Good morning, Sara. You look pretty good today. I do believe you have dimples in those cheeks when you smile." Dr. Maxwell stood in the doorway with his warm, friendly smile, squinting his eyes.

Sara turned when she heard his voice and her half smile changed to a scowl that wrinkled the bandage on her forehead. "Good morning, did you bring me a mirror?" she asked impatiently. This was the moment she'd been waiting for all this time. She was edgy and wanted to know if she'd remember the face . . . her face. Would the reflection in the glass unlock the door to her memories? When the knowledge that was locked away somewhere in her brain was released, would she be prepared to face her past? Instinctively she felt there was something back there that she was afraid of.

Sara's impatience didn't budge the smile from the doctor's lips. He knew how important this was to her; he only hoped it would help her. If it didn't, could she endure it? He couldn't let her know how worried he was about all the ramifications of her not remembering. He withdrew a hand mirror from one of the large pockets in his white coat. "I never break a promise if I can help it. Now, remember, you still have some bruises, but I assure you they will fade in time. If the face you see in the mirror isn't familiar, try not to be too disappointed. Just remember what I've

told you. Don't force it; your memory will return on its own."
He walked over to her chair and handed her the mirror.

Sara's hand trembled as she reached for the glass. What if the face wasn't familiar? What would she do then? But she had to find out, she couldn't stand not knowing much longer. Gulping some air into lungs that felt constricted, she closed her eyes and brought the mirror up in front of her face.

Slowly opening her eyes, the first thing she saw was the small bandage over the cut on her forehead. Almond-shaped, amber-colored eyes stared back at her. The dark yellow eyes flecked with brown looked frightened. The long blond hair was pulled back away from the face. Sara found herself looking at an attractive stranger but not anyone she knew. Bursting into tears, she threw the mirror away from her and buried the strange face in her hands.

Dr. Maxwell kneeled beside her, placing comforting arms around her shoulders. "Sara, give yourself some time. I told you it might not be an overnight process."

She looked up into his sympathetic and gentle eyes. "Time!" she screamed. "What does time mean when you don't even know your own face! Can't you understand? Who am I? I don't know that face. She's—I'm a stranger." Her sobs choked her, then she moaned. "It's been twelve long days. In another week I'll be leaving here with two strangers, Roarke and myself."

The doctor helped Sara over to her bed. She sat down and slumped over, wringing her hands together in her lap, her sobs shaking the bed. He sat on the bed beside her with his arm around her, holding her close. He let her cry for a little while longer then took her tear-streaked face in his hands. "Come on, Joe! It's time to pull yourself together. You know you'll remember soon. It's not as hopeless as you think. Haven't you remembered some things that have happened?"

Sara looked into the doctor's eyes, resentment, frustration, and fear filling hers. "Remember? How can you call it remembering when those damned flashes come and go so fast that I can't even hold on to them for a few seconds. Do you know what it's like to wake up in the morning not knowing who you are? People walk on tiptoes around me as though I'm crazy. The nurses spoonfeed me information, afraid to say too much and afraid to say too little. And Roarke! God, I don't know who to feel sorrier for, him or me. He comes in each day with that defensive look in his eyes, answering some of my questions but not volunteering any details about our life together."

Sara's hands shook and tears cascaded down her still slightly bruised cheeks. She could feel Dr. Maxwell pat her shoulder in an attempt to comfort her. Her head began to ache and the pain intensified with every sob that shook her body. "I can't stand much more. I'm going home soon. I'll be going home with Roarke." Sara chuckled bitterly through her tears. "Home. I don't even know where home is or what it looks like. Roarke has to take home a wife who's incapable of sharing anything with him. Dear God, what's going to happen to me?" She hung her head and the anguished sobs wracked her body.

The doctor took hold of one of her hands that she had folded into fists of frustration. "Sara, I don't know how you feel, it would be stupid of me to say I did. But there's one thing you must understand and remember—you had a severe blow on the head. Your body is in the process of healing itself and all this takes time. While your body is healing, there's not much energy left in you for big emotional battles. I know this is going to be hard to do, but you must accept the situation. Once your body is healed, you'll have the energy you need to explore all your feelings and flashes of memory."

Sara grabbed for the tissues sitting on the table beside her bed. After several attempts to pull herself together, she finally succeeded. "I didn't mean to come apart at the seams, but it's just so damn frustrating and I'm scared!"

Dr. Maxwell stood up and sighed, then smiled at Sara. He recognized the core of steel that Sara possessed as strength, even if she didn't. "Listen, in three months time you'll invite me to dinner and we'll laugh about all this. Just give yourself time. That's the magic prescription I have for you—time." He bent over and placed a gentle kiss on her bandaged forehead.

A dimple played momentarily on Sara's cheek. "What if . . ."

He held up his hand to stop her. "No 'what-ifs,' young lady. We'll cross all the 'what-ifs' when we come to them. Why don't you try to take a nap and I'll see you this evening." He watched Sara awkwardly climb under the covers. The heavy cast on her foot wouldn't be changed for a light walking cast for several more weeks and her side was still sore. He knew she was not only emotionally upset but physically uncomfortable. She had more courage under the circumstances than she realized. He winked as he turned to leave. "See you later, Joe." Sara's weak laughter followed him out of the room.

Once out in the corridor, Ted Maxwell paused and leaned against the wall. He was becoming very fond of Sara and his heart ached to see her so frustrated and disheartened. He only hoped that what he told her would come true. He shook his head and walked down the hall to answer his insistent beeper.

CHAPTER THREE

Sara gazed into the mirror every chance she had. She came to
know the reflected face very well, not because of any memories
but because she studied it so intently. Sara didn't think she was
being conceited in feeling that she was attractive. Her long ash
blond hair with its hint of natural curl was brushed back and
held with combs. The dark-amber eyes, shot through with
brown, changed their intensity with her moods. The tip of her
nose was slightly tilted, and her mouth was full and soft. When
she smiled, straight white teeth peeked through pink lips and
dimples appeared under her high-boned cheeks.

Sighing, she turned the mirror over and laid it on the bed. She
could feel her eyes smarting from the salty tears that were gathering on her lashes. *Damn,* she thought bitterly, *no matter how
often I study that face, it means nothing to me.* Clumsily she
crawled out of bed and grasped at her crutches. She had to
somehow escape this feeling of being trapped in a stranger's
body.

She limped around the room and her mind whirled with the
thoughts that not only was she trapped in a stranger's body but
was married to a stranger. Regardless of how often she saw
Roarke, there was no recognition, no familiarity. Their develop-
ing relationship was not one of continuing intimacy derived from
years of being together but from her viewpoint was new and
frightening. It seemed to her that Roarke and she were destined
to remain strangers because all they had in common was a past

she couldn't remember. She kept hoping that he would lift his obstinate veil of reluctancy to talk about their marriage, but she was unsuccessful in drawing him from behind it.

To add to her unhappy muddle of emotions, she conversely found herself looking forward to his visits with breathless expectancy. Not only did she want to remember him because he was her link to the past, but she was becoming curious about the physical side of their relationship.

When he would lean over and kiss her gently on the lips, the soft pressure would start a tingling that was both exciting and confusing. The slightest touch of his hand left a burning sensation on her flesh. If his eyes rested on her lovingly, her heart would begin to pound with the promise his look held. His very nearness seemed to awaken desire in her. She was afraid of how her body automatically remembered and responded to him, but when he left her, the arousal would be replaced with confusion. Tomorrow she would be going home with Roarke, and the thought of being alone with him intrigued and frightened her.

She was trying to follow Ted Maxwell's advice to give herself time, but sometimes she just couldn't control her agitation. And these were the times she paced around her room, limping on the crutches, ungainly in her attempt to run away from herself.

The new memory . . . her new memory, she thought possessively, of Roarke's visit last night brought tears to her eyes. Almost bouncing into the room, he had taken her into his arms, kissed her lightly on the lips and said, "Honey, I'm sorry I didn't get here to see you this morning."

Smiling and trying to ignore the tingling flesh of her lips where his had touched them, she teased him. "That's okay, your flowers were a fairly decent replacement. I really don't expect you to be here all the time. I feel sure you have more important things to do than come to this hospital to visit me."

At his crestfallen look she quickly added, "It would be nice if you could be here all the time, but I know you're busy, Roarke."

31

Her reassurance brought a pleased look to his face and his eyes glowed warmly. Placing his arm around her waist, he helped her to the chair by the window. "I'm glad you feel that way. I would be here all the time if I could be. We're all so excited about you coming home. Martha and Bradley have the entire house torn apart, getting it ready for your homecoming. It's going to be so wonderful to have you there, close by me again." He paused, cleared his throat, then continued. "It's so beautiful at home, the spring weather has been perfect and all the flowers are in bloom. Wait till you see it, the tulips you planted are gorgeous and the magnolia trees are ready to burst open." He kneeled beside her. "Are you eager to go home, darling?"

Sara looked into the clear blue eyes and mixed with the awe she felt over the fact that this man was her husband, she experienced a twinge of her now familiar companion, the fear that was with her constantly. "It sounds so beautiful, Roarke, but I don't think eager is quite the word. It's terrible not to remember people and things that have been so important in your life. Do Martha and Bradley know I don't remember them?"

Ignoring her plaintive question, he continued. "Your room is bright and beautiful, just waiting for your presence to complete the decor."

"What a nice thing to say, Roarke." Wistfully she turned her face away from him. "I'm sorry, but I don't remember anything about our home or our room."

Roarke slowly straightened up, dropped her hands, and gazed out the window. "It's . . . it's your room, Sara, not ours. I . . . ah . . . we . . . Ted Maxwell and I thought it would be better if you had your own room. You'll . . . you'll rest better." Glancing over his shoulder, he said in a low voice, "I'll be just across the hall from you."

Sara dropped her eyes and a small "oh" escaped her lips.

Roarke continued to stare outside and the silence between them lengthened oppressively. Sara felt almost compulsive in her need to fill the void. She struggled to think of something to say then recalled an incident from earlier in the day. "Roarke, I'd like to ask you something. This afternoon when the nurse mentioned about packing to go home, I had one of those crazy flashes of memory." She stopped abruptly when he pivoted around. A grim expression distorted his features.

His back stiffened and he asked tautly, "Just what is it you think you remember?"

Confused by his tone of voice and his threatening posture, Sara answered quietly, "I saw myself walking out of a house with suitcases. I was crying as I put them in the trunk of a car."

His brows lowered over his darkened eyes. "You were going on a trip." The words were clipped short.

"On a trip? Why was I crying so hard?"

Roarke looked out the window again and mumbled, "You hate good-byes."

Sara shook her head with disbelief. "Roarke, please look at me. No one cries that way just because they hate to say good-bye. I can hardly believe that."

His eyes seemed to pierce her heart. "Believe what you want, Sara, you always did. I have to leave now. I'll see you tomorrow."

Sara stared at the empty doorway for several minutes after he disappeared through it. Finally she began to weep from sheer tension and confoundment. Was there no way to keep their relationship on an even keel? How could a man be so thoughtful and sensitive about some things and yet at the same time be insensitive to her predicament? It had to be all her fault somehow. She always seemed to ask him the wrong question or say the wrong thing. But what, she anguished, was wrong with what she said or asked?

The chatter of a group of nurses walking past her door caught her attention and brought her mind back to the present. Her arms were aching and she realized she had been frantically limping around the small room as though really trying to run away.

How could she leave the hospital to go home with Roarke? The hospital and especially Ted had come to represent a safe haven for her. She quivered at the thought of Ted abandoning her to Roarke. Ted was compassionate and understanding but Roarke—every time she mentioned the past, he shut her out. It was as though he were hiding something from her. She almost believed he didn't want her to remember. The thought of not remembering and spending the rest of her life not knowing who she was was too terrifying to think about.

Ted kept telling her that when she got home and into familiar surroundings that her memory would probably return quickly. But after not recognizing Roarke or herself, she held out little hope that their home would help bring back her memory.

Slumping into the chair, she threw the crutches down onto the floor and cringed as their sharp clatter broke the silence. The dejection that infused her mind with such hopelessness made her want to get up and run away. She looked down at the cast on her foot and a wry smile parted her lips. She turned her head to look outside. *Run away? Even if I knew where to run, how could I run?*

"Good morning, Sara. How are you today?" Ted came in the door shuffling several papers he held in his hands. "Isn't it beautiful out there?"

"Is it really? I think it's pretty scary."

"Come on now, what's the matter, Joe?"

"How can you ask such a dumb question, Ted? I'm sitting here watching all those people out there. Did you ever sit and wonder about other people's lives and what they're like? They all seem to know their destination . . . and I don't. They know they belong somewhere . . . and I don't."

"Sara, don't torture yourself like this. You do know who you are. You do know where you're going. You do belong."

Swinging around to face Ted, she said vehemently, "Where do I belong? Yes, I know my name, but what does that mean?

34

Nothing! You tell me I'm Roarke's wife, but do I belong with him? You sure can't tell by the way he acts."

Ted's hand reached out and brushed a stray strand of hair away from her face. Quietly he said, "Sara, I know you feel boxed in by your fear and the panic of not being able to remember. But you can't lose sight of the fact that Roarke is panicked and has fears too. He cares about you. I know he cares about you. I saw him while you were unconscious and in Intensive Care. The man was practically inconsolable. He stayed at this hospital for three days, barely eating or sleeping. You have to snap out of this. I know you're going to be all right. Now you have to believe it."

Shrugging her shoulders, she smiled plaintively. "Maybe you're right, Ted. I'll try harder but I just wish . . ."

"Wish what?"

"That . . . that Roarke would try harder."

"It will be easier when you're home and that's what I came in here to tell you. You're going home today."

Sara jumped up from her chair, then fell back into it. She could feel the blood draining from her face. "Why today? I thought you said I wouldn't be going home until tomorrow." Her voice was shaking but not as badly as her stomach.

"I don't have any reason to keep you here for another day. You can do the rest of your recuperating at home better than you can do it in this hospital. It had to come sometime, Sara. Once you're out of this regimented atmosphere, you'll be surprised at how much faster you'll get better."

"When do I leave?" Sara asked in a quavering voice. She wondered if she would be able to move. Her body felt leaden, and she had to swallow to keep down the sickening feeling in her stomach.

"I called Roarke when I went over your records this morning. He'll be here shortly to sign your release and take you home." Ted went over to her and crouched down in front of the chair and took both her ice cold hands into his warmer ones. "Sara, this will be better for you. You can't hide for the rest of your life. You know that, don't you?" He waited for her response and when she nodded reluctantly, he continued, "The longer you put things off and try to hide from them, the harder it's going to be for you."

Sara lifted her head up to face him. "I guess you're right, but I can't help being frightened." Her lower lip trembled as she spoke and she bit it to keep it still. She grasped Ted's hands as though they were her link to life.

Ted smiled fondly at her. "There's nothing wrong with being frightened. Everyone is at one time or another. It just shows you're alive and feeling."

Sara glanced up at the big round clock above the door and was startled to see Roarke standing in the doorway. His face was marred by an angry scowl and Sara felt a twinge of guilt. She didn't know why he should be angry or why she should feel guilty. Ignoring his anger, Sara smiled tremulously. "Good morning, Roarke."

Roarke nodded his head in acknowledgment of her greeting but never took his eyes off Ted's kneeling figure nor the fact that Ted was holding her hands. "I understood you were to come home today." His tone was barely civil. He walked over to Sara's bed and laid down the clothes he was carrying in his arms.

Ted dropped Sara's hands and stood up. "Yes, that's right. She is going home. I have papers for you to sign and an appointment to set up for Sara; then she can leave." Ted picked up the papers from the bed that he had brought in with him. "It would be easier if we did this in my office. A nurse will be coming to help Sara pack her things." He turned back to Sara, who was still sitting in the chair with her hands clenched together. "Well, Sara, we're going to miss you around here. But you know I'm just a phone call away. I'll make an appointment with Roarke to see you next week." Ted winked at Sara and walked to the door. "Take care . . . Joe."

With a quizzical glance at Sara, Roarke joined Ted at the door and they left together, the tall sophisticated, handsome man whom everyone told her was her husband but was a stranger and the big husky doctor who had become her friend.

Roarke waited patiently while the nurse helped Sara get settled in the front seat of the car then walked around to the driver's side. Nervously Sara tucked her lightweight coat against her legs and kept her eyes averted from Roarke's. Panic was trying to grip her senses and she battled with herself to hold it at bay. She gasped at the sound of the powerful motor coming to life and held on to the armrest as Roarke deftly maneuvered the car and merged with the heavy traffic.

"Why are you so nervous, Sara? You never used to worry about my driving."

Sara glanced over at the face of the man beside her. His profile was stonelike, and his full attention was on the road in front of them. But the rigidity of his features mystified her and a sense of irritation began to permeate her panic and dilute it. "Your driving has nothing to do with me being nervous. Roarke, don't you understand what's wrong with me? I'm scared. I'm so damn scared I can hardly talk." Sara twisted her body in the seat and faced Roarke. "You act like you don't want me to go home with you. From the minute I saw you in the doorway of my room, you've acted as though you're angry because I'm coming home."

He glanced at her then swept his eyes back to the traffic. "What gave you that crazy idea? Of course I want you home."

Swinging around to face the front of the car, she folded her arms across her chest. "I don't think my feelings are so crazy. If you didn't want to be inconvenienced by having to drive me, you could have sent a taxi." She chuckled bitterly. "Of course you'd have had to tell the driver where we live, since I don't remember!"

His head whipped around toward her, "Sara, stop it right now! Don't be so dramatic."

Turning to him again, she exploded, "Dramatic? Don't I have

37

good reason to be dramatic? I'm scared! I don't understand you at all, Roarke."

She watched a twisted smile flicker across his lips. "Come off it, Sara!"

Sara wanted to scream with rage. What was wrong with him? They were fighting and she didn't know why. *Things are never going to work out,* she thought miserably. *He's moody, unpredictable, and unfeeling. Regardless of what Ted says, Roarke doesn't care or he wouldn't treat me like this.* Clamping her mouth tightly shut, she faced the front of the car and tried to ignore him and her feelings.

By the time they pulled into a long circular driveway, her head was whirling from all her grim thoughts. The car came to a jarring stop and Roarke opened his door, got out of the car, and came around to her side. "We're home, Sara." Roarke said wearily as he opened her door. Holding out his hand to her, he reached over and touched her elbow. Shrinking away from him, she watched as his face shadowed with irritation. "What's wrong now?"

Suddenly she knew she couldn't stay with this man. Husband or not, the situation was intolerable. If she weren't insane, his lack of understanding and impatience would soon drive her there. Her fear was full-blown and beyond her control. She shrunk farther away from his outstretched hand and whispered gutturally, "Take me back to the hospital . . . now!"

Roarke leaned into the open door and grabbed her arm. "Sara, what in the hell are you talking about? Get out of the car and let's go into the house."

Through gritted teeth she gnashed out, "I'm not going into that house with you. Take me back to Ted Maxwell."

With a sardonic chuckle Roarke straightened up. "Oh, Sara," he shook his head, "you've done it again. Ted Maxwell! I really thought for once you were being honest with me. I must admit you almost had me convinced. It's all just another game, isn't it, Sara? God, Sara, when is one man going to be enough for you?"

Sara was flabbergasted. What is he talking about? A game? How could he think she was playing any game? But the bitterness in his eyes was unmistakable and the contempt in his voice lashed her like a whip. She opened her mouth but couldn't say a word. The anger washed out of her as her befuddlement grew.

A middle-aged man came out of the house. His face was wrinkled from the smile that seemed to split it in half. He walked over to the car as Sara unwillingly struggled from the seat. "Mrs. Alexander, it's so nice to have you home. I'm Bradley. If there's anything you need, anything, please just ask." Still smiling, he turned away and walked to the back of the car to get her bag.

Sara clutched her crutches tightly as she lumbered toward the house. Roarke was directly behind her and she was angry from the thought that he was trying to guard her, to keep her from running away. Peevishly she thought, *Does he really think I could get away? He's so close to my heels, if he's not careful, he'll trip over my feet.*

Glancing up at the entrance of the house, she saw a heavy-set woman standing in the doorway holding her apron to her eyes. Sara realized with a start that the woman was crying, and before she knew what was happening, the woman swept her into a tight embrace.

"Oh, Miss Sara, it's so good to have you home! I know you don't remember me, but I just had to hug you to make sure you were really here." The woman held Sara at arm's length from her motherly form and looked at her critically. "You're too skinny, but I can fix that. Mr. Roarke, this child is fairly dropping. You take her upstairs to her room and let her rest. I'll bring you some lunch later," she said to Sara as she once more embraced her as though Sara were a child.

Sara looked to Roarke for help and saw the veil of contempt over his eyes. Before she could say a word, Roarke picked her up in his arms and carried her up the wide, curving staircase to a room off to the right of the long, carpeted hall.

He dropped her on the bed, went back to the door, and closed

39

it firmly. He walked back to her, stopped at the edge of the bed, and ran his eyes up and down her body.

Lying rigidly on top of the quilted bedspread, Sara felt stripped naked physically and emotionally by his openly leering gaze and she was frightened. What was he up to now? She shuddered a little and inched her body away from him. Her heart started pounding rapidly and the palms of her hands were sweating.

"Let's get one thing straight right now, Sara." He seemed to spit the words from his mouth. "I will not take you back to the hospital and especially not to Ted Maxwell. You are my wife and you will stay right here. If you want to play a game, Sara, you will not play it with anyone else. This game will be solitaire."

His sarcasm cut through her, but for one second Sara thought she saw hurt in those deep blue eyes. She must have imagined it, because they were still viewing her very coldly.

"Roarke," she whispered shakily. She couldn't control the trembling in her body. "Please, listen to me."

He kept his eyes on her face, ignoring her shaking body. "What can you possibly have to say to me?"

"I don't understand what you're talking about. What game?" Tears glistened in her eyes. "Please, Roarke, don't turn on me like this. I haven't done anything to deserve it."

"Forget it, Sara. I'm used to all your feminine wiles and ploys for sympathy. You can beg and plead with me all you like, but it won't do you any good. I'm probably the only man in the world who knows what you're really like." He stalked out of the room, his back rigid with fury.

Sara turned over, buried her face in the pillow, pounded it with her fists, and cried wildly. *What has happened? Why is Roarke behaving like this? Does he really intend to try to keep me a prisoner? Was this how he acted all the time? If he did, why in the hell had she married him?* Wailing out loud, she moaned, "What do I do now?"

* * *

Groggy, Sara heard a soft tapping on the door. Propping herself up on one elbow, she looked around the room, awareness slowly replacing sleep. With a rising sense of panic, she realized someone was in the room with her.

"I didn't like to wake you up, Miss Sara, but I figured you might be hungry, so I brought you a tray."

Sara looked in the direction of the soft voice and saw Martha's round form silhouetted in the light coming through the window. Everything had a strange dreamlike quality and Sara struggled to overcome the eerie feeling.

"Thank you, Martha," she responded quietly as she swung her feet off the bed and limped over to the table in front of the balcony window. Sipping at a cup of coffee, she glanced at Martha standing near her. Her arms were crossed over her ample bosom and she was studying Sara's face intently.

"Is there something wrong, Martha?" Sara finally broke the silence, mystified and a little uncomfortable under the woman's scrutiny.

Clearing her throat, Martha answered softly, "Maybe you could answer that better than me, Miss Sara. But I was just standing here thanking our lucky stars that you're home and getting well. That was a horrible accident you had."

Startled by Martha's response to her question, Sara asked, "Why would you think I could answer my question better than you, Martha? Roarke told you I have amnesia and can't remember anything that happened before I woke up in the hospital. I'm pleased you're glad I'm here, but I have the feeling that something isn't right and you know what it is."

Martha started moving toward the door. "Miss Sara, I've taken care of Mr. Roarke for years, and when you came to this house as a bride, you were like a daughter to me. I couldn't love you two any more if you were my flesh and blood. I've tried never to interfere in your lives and I'm not about to start now. This has been a terrible time in this house, and now I pray that it gets back to normal. Anytime you want to talk or if you want to know something, just ask me. I'll tell you everything I can. It's just so wonderful to have you home."

Sara was surprised to see Martha reach up and wipe a tear off her cheek and was speechless as the woman left the room. What a strange conversation!

Her coffee cup clattered against the saucer. Why did any conversation she have with anyone who had anything to do with her past have to be so cryptic? It seemed to her that she had more questions than answers. No one seemed to want to help her remember, not Roarke and not Martha.

Sara pushed her chair away from the table slowly, got to her feet, and hobbled around the room. Her habit of pacing the small hospital room to relieve her tension unconsciously took over. The one thought that kept surfacing through her tumultuous thinking was Roarke's behavior today. From the moment he had appeared in her doorway at the hospital, he had been an enigma. He had been barely civil and almost surly at times, withdrawn and uncommunicative at others. His anger was unexplainable and uncalled for. She felt he had made several oblique references to her past, but what did they mean? What kind of a person had she been? If only he'd sit down and calmly tell her what their life together had been like and what kind of a person she was, then she would understand him. After all, he admitted he was the only man who knew what she was really like!

Sitting on the edge of the bed, she rubbed her hand over her eyes. *He said so many perplexing things to me, if only I knew why,* she thought. *Am I really a man-chaser who plays games? Oh, my God, surely that isn't true!* She curled up on the bed and put her head on the pillow, tears trickling down her cheeks. *Am I the sort of woman who throws herself at men and is this why Roarke is so contemptuous and bitter toward me? When he saw Ted holding my hands, that seemed to set off his anger. Does he have reason to accuse me as he did?*

Sitting up, Sara wiped her face with her fingertips and looked around the room. *I have to quit weeping at the drop of a problem,* she reflected. *I have to get my mind off this mess for a little while, or I will go stark raving mad.* Until someone would tell her about her past or her memory came back on its own, she was a prisoner in this house and in this room. More than that, she was a prisoner of her own mind, walls of forgetfulness blocking out her past.

CHAPTER FOUR

"Sara, where are you?" the deep voice demanded.

Struggling with her balance, Sara peered around the edge of the closet door. "I'm here, just a second."

Roarke! It was Roarke calling her, she thought nervously. She was hoping against hope he would leave her alone until she could strengthen herself and figure out what approach to take with him.

"What on earth are you doing?" Roarke asked as she came into view.

She limped over to the chaise longue and sat down, hesitating until she felt a little more composed before answering him. "I was tired of lying in bed with nothing to do. My curiosity got the better of me"—she shrugged her shoulders—"so I decided to look around. Are all those clothes really mine? That closet is huge and just jammed with beautiful things."

Roarke glanced over toward the closet and nodded his head. "Yes, they're all yours. You love clothes, obviously." He took a pack of cigarettes out of his shirt pocket, shook one out, and lit it while his eyes lowered to concentrate on the glowing end.

Sara watched the flame from the lighter flicker quickly across his face, the plains and ridges of his cheeks prominent in the flash of light. His black hair was a little unruly and one strand fell across his forehead. Then he looked up and their eyes locked. Sara's breath stopped as the blueness of his eyes seemed to draw her into their depths. There seemed to be no way she could break the spell. Several heart-wrenching seconds drew out as he studied her face. Sara could feel her lips part slightly and finally, with a shuddering breath, she lowered her eyelids.

"Sara, I hope you'll accept my apology for this morning." Roarke's voice, even though it was low, seemed to roar in her ears, the waves of sounds beating against her eardrums. "I can't give you any explanation right now, but I realize I was overreacting to what was possibly an innocent situation—"

"Possibly innocent!" she interrupted. "I don't believe this, Roarke. Even your apology is qualified!"

Holding his hand up, he appealed, "Please, let me finish, Sara. I don't want to fight with you. That's not why I came in here. I tried to think this through today while you were resting, and I've come to the conclusion we can't continue this way. It's not going to help you get better and I certainly don't want to feel responsible for that." He put the cigarette to his mouth and drew the smoke deeply into his lungs. Exhaling, his face secret behind a fog of smoke, his breath swirling it in the air, he continued. "I do want you to get well, Sara. I want to help anyway I can. I know this isn't easy for you, but it isn't easy for me either. I'm not asking for your sympathy, but I do need some understanding from you . . . and a little patience too. I feel helpless and confused." Pausing, he took another drag from his cigarette.

Sara could feel her heart begin to swell. He seemed so vulnerable. Then the whole irrationality of his words took hold. She spoke softly but adamantly. "Roarke, I have felt sorry for both of us. But, I have to admit, I don't understand you. I don't remember you or anything else and you don't seem to want to help me. How can I understand you and have patience with you when I don't have either for myself? I tell you I'm afraid, and you ignore me. I beg for you to tell me about our past, and you put a wall between us and I don't know why. I plead for understanding from you and feel your contempt. Don't you think it's ironic that you'd ask me for understanding and patience? Understanding about what? Patience for what? You have the advantage. You know why you need my understanding and patience, but I don't remember why I need yours, and . . . and I do."

She could feel her voice rising with each sentence and stopped short, catching her breath. She put her hand over her mouth and stared at Roarke as he moved toward the door. Was he going to leave her? Had she gone too far?

But instead of leaving he walked over to her and sat down on the foot of the chaise. "Sara, I know this is hard for you. The whole situation is terrible, and you must be very frightened, but so am I."

"You're frightened?" She sat up and leaned toward him. "What are you frightened of? Why won't you explain things to me? You keep telling me you'll help me anyway you can, so why don't you?"

Jumping to his feet, Roarke started pacing. "I do want to help you but you're not listening to what I've really been saying . . . *anyway I can.*"

"That's what Martha said to me this morning, word for word. Why is everyone being so cryptic? What in the hell is going on? What is so frightening to everyone in this house?" She leaned back and closed her eyes. Sagging under the weight of her thoughts, she gasped. "Maybe you're all looking on my amnesia as a blessing. Is that it, Roarke?" Sitting up brusquely, her eyes flew open wide and she cried out, "What is it you don't want me to remember and everyone is afraid I will? For God's sake, Roarke, did I kill someone?" She flung her hands over her face as she tried to stop the tears that stung her eyes.

She felt her hands being pried away from her cheeks and, opening her eyes, saw Roarke kneeling beside her. "Sara, don't be so foolish. Of course you didn't kill anyone." He stood up and turned his back to her. "Maybe I do feel a little that your amnesia is a blessing." His voice was anguished and she waited breathlessly for him to continue. "But, believe me, I only want good to come of it. Ted Maxwell says you'll remember everything on your own and I've decided to take my chances and wait for that to happen. In the meantime, short of telling you all the details of your past, I'll help you all I can. I'll help you get back in touch with yourself. I'll take you to some of your favorite places when you're well enough to get around. I promise you I won't block your remembering." He turned back to face her and looked deeply into her eyes. "But I want you to remember about us on your own."

Later that night, watching the moonlight shine obliquely through her window, slanting a solid path across the carpet, Sara drifted between wakefulness and sleep. Her mind replayed her conversation with Roarke and she sleepily wondered if their truce would last. They never seemed to be able to have a lucid, calm conversation. Their times together were always fraught with high-powered emotion.

She just wished she knew what Roarke was frightened of. What was in their past that he was afraid to tell her? He still hadn't told her why he had been so angry when he came into her hospital room, but she knew it had something to do with Ted Maxwell. Sighing, she rolled over onto her side. Roarke's accusation of her not being happy with one man still rang in her head. Maybe this is what he didn't want her to remember, that she liked men and this had given them problems in their marriage. Maybe she was a flirt or worse! Her half-closed eyes flew open. That just couldn't be . . . just couldn't be!

The next three weeks crawled with miserable slowness. To alleviate some of the boredom, Bradley and Roarke had brought a TV set to her room and, while she enjoyed some of the programs, most of her time in front of the set was spent in mindless inattention.

She could feel her strength returning more and more each day. Martha tried on several occasions to convince her to go downstairs, but Sara put her off. Her security, what little she had, was bound up with the four walls of her room. Ted hadn't wanted her to go up and down the stairs more than once a day anyway, so she used this as a partial excuse.

The truce between Roarke and herself remained in effect. Sara would catch him looking at her with a speculative expression sometimes, but they didn't have any more arguments. They established a routine of dining together in her room when Roarke was at home.

These encounters with him left her in turmoil. The truce may have eased some of the tensions between them, but it caused new tensions in her. While he wasn't the same loving man she had first seen in the hospital, his charm and charisma embraced her. He didn't initiate any intimacy between them, but when he'd casually touch her hand or kiss her on the forehead when he left to go to his own room, her body would ache with unfulfilled longings—the longing to have him hold her close, to touch her, the longing to make her feel wanted. Even though she struggled against these yearnings, the struggle was in vain. She'd lie in bed at night imagining he was holding her in his arms. She didn't permit her imaginings to go any further. The constant battle with these feelings made her sick with contempt for herself because they made her recall his accusations of other men in her life and made her wonder what kind of woman she had been. Sometimes Sara was glad when Roarke couldn't make it home for dinner and she would eat alone, content with her own company without having Roarke's presence to stir up her ambiguous feelings about him.

She still couldn't remember anything and now disturbing dreams began to plague her. One night she roused groggily, her heart pounding. She knew she had been dreaming, but a deep, ominous sound had filtered into the dream, mixing with the all-pervasive feeling of fear. As her lids began to slowly fall over her sleep-glazed eyes, again she heard the sound and, panic stricken, her eyes wide with terror, her breath coming in deep gulps, she clutched the blanket to her chin. Then a low chuckle started at the base of her throat and rose to escape through her lips. It was a dog! That's what she heard, a dog barking some-where. How silly for her to fear the shadows and sounds that came in the night.

Sleepily wondering whose dog was barking, she rolled over onto her side, dozed off and drifted into a dream room. She walked through the mist that made the perimeter of the room seem shrouded in fog and over to a brightly lit couch and chair where Roarke was standing beside a huge box wrapped with green satin ribbon and a huge bow covering the lid of the box, all shimmering under the glow of a nearby lamp.

"Roarke, what a beautiful bow!" She clapped her hands to-gether in childish delight. "I love green, but what's in the box? Come on, darling, why a present? It's not my birthday or any-thing."

Roarke smiled and took her hand. "Just wait; you'll see what's in it in a minute." His arms slipped around her waist, moving slowly, caressing her side as his hand stroked her back. "Can't you guess what's in the box, Sara?"

Sara snuggled closer into his arms, tore her eyes from his face, and looked again at the box, shimmering, glowing white and green on the floor at her feet. "Roarke, there's something in it! Something alive! The box is moving!"

The whimper emanating from the box made Sara shift her body in Roarke's arms and suddenly she once again found her-self awake, lying in bed, blinking her eyes, bemused by the dream, but instead of fear and panic, a warm feeling of security filled her senses.

But it was the pulse-thudding, stomach-turning, paralyzing nightmares that dominated her sleep and, in the middle of the night, she would wake up drenched with perspiration. In her dreams screaming people pursued her as she ran blindly toward some unknown person who seemed to represent safety. In her dreams her movements were always in slow motion, and the feeling of terror pervaded her being, a living entity taking over her soul.

She mentioned these nightmares to Ted when she saw him on one of her check-ups. He put his hand on her shoulder as she sat up on the examination table. "Do you want some sleeping pills? I don't like to prescribe them, but in this case, I don't want you to become ill from lack of sleep either."

Sara shook her head, "No, Ted, thanks anyway. I don't have that much trouble sleeping, although I hate the dreams. Sometimes they're so scary, it's as though something awful is going to happen and I'm powerless to stop it. It's just like everything else—I don't seem to have any control over my life, awake or sleeping!"

"Now, wait a minute, Sara. They are exactly what they are—dreams, nothing else. They're not any forecast of doom. You're frustrated because you're not remembering that much yet. That's the only thing these dreams mean—your frustration. Have you discussed them with Roarke?"

Sara hung her head. "No, I haven't told him. I . . . I don't want to worry him if there's nothing to worry about."

Ted went to the door of the examination room and opened it. "There really isn't. You're healing fast and in no time you won't be needing me anymore."

That night when she woke up, sobbing and shaking uncontrollably from the fearful dream, Sara remembered Ted's words and prayed they were true.

Nervously she waited for Ted to come into the room. She didn't know if she was happy or not about having the cast removed, but it would eliminate her excuse to stay in her room.

"Are you ready, Sara?" Ted's jovial voice boomed from the doorway.

"No, but I don't have much choice, do I?" Sara answered, glancing over at the small, shiny electric saw laying on a table beside her.

When the buzzing noise began, she closed her eyes and turned her head.

"All done. You can open your eyes now."

Sara looked down at the wrinkled skin of her foot. Twisting it around, at first slowly then with a little more speed, Sara laughed. "It feels so light! But it feels so good, a little stiff but no pain. Are you sure it's going to hold me up? I don't know how to walk without a cast. I've used crutches for so long, I'm almost afraid to try to walk without them."

Ted smiled broadly and helped her to her feet. "Come on, walk with me into my office. Go easy now." He put his arm around her waist and slowly they walked together into Ted's private office.

Lowering herself down onto the couch, Sara straightened her leg out in front of her. "It held, Ted, it's really okay. I could run if I wanted to, couldn't I?"

Ted looked at her strangely. "Run?" he asked. "No, I don't think I'd try to run just yet. You're going to be using a cane for a few weeks to take some of the weight off that foot." He paused. "Why would you want to run, Sara?"

Sara glanced around the room, a little uncomfortable. *Why did I say such a dumb thing?* She cringed inwardly. "I really didn't mean it literally, Ted. Although, to be perfectly honest with you, I've had times when I've wanted to run. I guess no one knows until they've gone through it how terrible it is not to have a past. Everyone has memories and people they can relate to but . . . but I don't."

"Still nothing, Sara?"

"Oh," she sighed, "I have mental flashes occasionally of things but nothing that I can tie together and say, yes, I remember that."

Ted sat on the couch beside her. "Sara, I've been thinking, I have this friend who's a psychiatrist. Maybe he could help you."

Startled, she cried out, "Psychiatrist! Do you think I'm crazy?"

Quickly Ted reassured her. "No, no, Sara. Nothing like that. But have you ever thought there might be something in your past that you're afraid to remember? Or that you just don't want to remember? There's a slight possibility your amnesia is psychosomatic."

Sara grabbed Ted's arm, clenching it tightly. "You don't believe me either. I've had the feeling Roarke doesn't believe me and now you. This isn't a game I'm playing, you know." She winced at the word *game*.

Ted put his hand over hers. "Sara, calm down. Of course I believe you have amnesia. I was just trying to figure out what might be the reason it's lasted this long. And Roarke believes you. Why would you say such a thing? We're both trying to help you. I'm sorry I've upset you, my dear. That's the last thing I'd ever want to do."

Relaxing a little, Sara murmured, "I know, Ted. I'm just so . . . so jumpy. It seems like it's taking me forever to get well."

Ted patted her cheek. "Sara, you're going to be fine. Try not to worry so much. I still say one of these days, like a bolt out of the blue, your memory will return and everything will fall into place for you."

At home in her bedroom Sara timidly walked around, leaning heavily on the cane. She tried not to dwell on Ted's words, they scared her so badly. If only she could talk things over with Roarke, but she knew she couldn't. They were fine as long as they chatted casually, but she just couldn't tell him her fears.

Slowly she made her way to the huge window leading to her balcony. The small area was a shining spot of consolation to her self-imposed isolation from the rest of the house. Breathing the fresh spring air, she drew it deeply into her lungs as she went over to the rail of the balcony. Leaning down and resting her chin in the palm of her hand, she closed her eyes, relishing the feeling of the sun on her face.

"Oh, how I love my flowers," she murmured low, and across the back of her closed lids a picture formed, the colors at first dull and muddy but, as she watched, they became brilliant, vivid, and alive.

It was she, kneeling down on the earth, prodding its warm firmness with a trowel, carefully digging around a bed of flowers.

"What on earth do you think I pay a gardener for, Sara?" It was Roarke's deep voice behind her, firm but filled with the sound of indulgent love.

She turned the upper portion of her body to face him. "Roarke, you know I love my flowers, how can I let someone else take care of them? They need my tender loving care!" She struggled to her feet and, as she leaned over to pick up the trowel, squealed in mock pain as she felt Roarke's fingers nip at the fleshy part of her buttock. "What are you doing, Roarke Alexander?"

"Just letting you know there's someone else who needs your tender loving care." And with deep laughter low in his chest, he swept her into his arms and started walking toward the house.

At a sound behind her, Sara turned and the vision cracked and splintered, falling away in tiny fragments to reveal Martha standing in the bedroom, her arms full of large tablets and carrying some sort of a small metal case clutched in one hand, followed by Bradley, balancing her lunch tray in his hands.

"What on earth . . . ?"

"Come in here, Miss Sara. I want to show you something."

She put the case down and opened one of the sketch pads and held it so Sara could see a drawing of a black puppy.

Sara sat down on the edge of the bed, taking the pad in her hands. "Martha, what a good sketch! Look at those eyes, they almost glow with life. Who did this? It's very good."

Martha chuckled. "The artist was you, Miss Sara. When you're steadier on your feet, you can come downstairs to your workroom. All your paints are there. In fact, your easel still stands in the corner, waiting for you. These are some of your sketch pads and I brought up the case with your charcoal, pencils, and some watercolors in it for you."

Sara looked up, moving her eyes slowly from the sketch she

53

held in front of her. "I did this?" she asked incredulously. "I paint? Why didn't you tell me sooner, Martha?"

"Because Mr. Roarke said the most important thing for you was rest and I agreed with him one hundred percent. I know you don't remember, but you were so dedicated to your painting that once you started something, you would work for hours on end, ignoring time, food, and even Mr. Roarke. And look at you right now"—Martha's eyes took in her thin body—"you're skinny as a rail. I couldn't have it on my conscience if you missed meals because you were too busy painting. But since Dr. Maxwell took that cast off your leg this morning, in a couple days you'll be as good as new, so I figured it was time to remind you of your drawing."

"Whoa, slow down, Martha," Sara chuckled. "You don't have to convince me that I'm too thin. And I agree with you, now that I'm able to get around, I probably will eat better." She tapped the sketch pad with her hand. "I really drew this?" she asked again, still a little amazed by this revelation.

Martha drew her shoulders up and lifted her chin proudly. "Indeed you did, young lady. In fact there are several of your paintings hanging in a gallery in Washington, D.C., at an amateur art exhibit. Mr. Roarke took Bradley and me to see them." Hastily Martha put her hand over her mouth and turned to Bradley. "Do you have the table set?" she asked almost brusquely.

Puzzled, Sara started to ask her what was wrong, but Martha interrupted her. "Please eat all your lunch, Miss Sara. I sure wouldn't want Dr. Maxwell to think I didn't feed you right and that it's my fault you're so skinny."

Patting her arm as she made her way past Martha, Sara said comfortingly, "Don't worry, Martha, I wouldn't let him blame you."

As she was leaving the room, Martha paused. "Oh, Miss Sara, Mr. Roarke called and said to expect him for dinner. So why don't you take a nice long rest and I'll fix up a special dinner to celebrate your cast coming off today."

Pushing open the sliding door, Sara grappled with the cane in one hand and the oversized tablet and pencils in the other. She didn't feel like sleeping; she felt too restless. Settling herself on the chaise, she placed the sketch pad on her lap. Flipping back the cover of the pad, she studied the blank paper. How did she start, she wondered, putting the pencil point against the paper. She frowned as nothing came into her mind then blinked her eyes.

Like thick clouds moving across the sky opening suddenly to reveal the blue behind them, a mist opened slowly in the middle of the paper and revealed blue water and brown sand. Sara watched spellbound as two figures materialized. The vision sharpened and she saw herself sitting on a beach beside Roarke, a huge sketch pad in her hands, her hair blowing in the light breeze.

"Come on, Roarke, hold still! I want to sketch you, darling. That dune and the dried grass behind you will be a wonderful background," she begged.

Roarke laughed, his eyes glowing and reflecting the sun. She was sketching madly, her hand moving so fast it was blurred. Following the trail of the piece of charcoal she held in her fingers were the lines of his face which was coming to life on the paper. Roarke leaned over and brushed a grain of sand off her nose and abruptly Sara was back on her balcony, stunned by the scenario she had envisioned. She reached up to her nose but shook her head.

Glancing down at the sketch pad, she was astounded to see Roarke's face staring back at her. *Did I draw this?* she wondered, absorbed with the sketch. She did draw it, the paper had been blank when she sat down, she was positive of that. Quickly ruffling the pages of the pad, she thought that maybe she had done it sometime before this, but the rest of the pages were bare also.

The thought of her flashback electrified her. Except for the one in the hospital when she remembered the pajamas, this was the strongest memory she had experienced yet. In a daze she studied the face drawn on the paper. *This isn't the Roarke I know,* she protested to herself. *I've never seen him look like this.* The eyes were soft and filled with love, the dark hair tousled on his head as though blown by a brisk wind. Lips curved in a sensuous smile that made her heart beat faster. She could almost feel those lips on hers.

Struggling to her feet, she made her way back into her room. *This isn't the way he is,* thought Sara bitterly. *This is a drawing of some younger Roarke I don't know.* She tore the sheet of paper out of the sketch pad and threw it across the room, where it landed on the floor near the door. She sat down at the table, her pencil tearing furiously at the paper. *This is what he looks like to me! This is what his marriage to me has done to him!* With each bitter thought her pencil slashed across the paper, and when she finally dropped the pencil on the table, the man drawn on the paper looked back at her—a handsome face with cold eyes glittering behind half-lowered lids, mouth closed in a firm line with furrows across the broad forehead and running alongside the straight, full lips.

She stooped over to pick up the drawing she had thrown on the floor then sat down on the bed, holding one in each hand. Tears trickled down her cheeks as she looked from one to the other. The first Roarke she had drawn was gentle and tender. This was the face of a man filled with love. This was the face of the man she must have loved. Her heart trembled at the thought.

A glance at the other Roarke revealed a hardened face staring back at her, a face she hadn't created just with her pencil but one she had helped create in real life. Suddenly the black pit of loneliness and fright she had become so familiar with yawned open and tried to swallow her. Tears shimmered in her eyes as the realization washed over her that she was really dependent on a man who didn't seem to care for her and wouldn't help her.

She was alone, friendless, parentless, with no one to turn to except Roarke.

Sara dropped the pad on the bed and tenderly held the single sheet with Roarke's loving face sketched on it. *If only,* she thought, *if only he would look at me like this again. I could love a man who looked like this.* Her fingertips traced the black lines of the picture's lips. *Oh, Roarke,* she wept inwardly, *I don't remember loving you, but how could I have not loved you. I don't remember what I was like then or how I turned you against me, but I'm not that way now. I'm a new person, and . . . and . . . I need you.*

A flush crept up her face. What in the world was the matter with her? She absently rubbed her forehead and placed the drawing back into the sketch pad. She went into the bathroom and turned the cold water on in the basin and splashed her face. She stared at her reflection in the mirror as she patted the towel against her cheeks. If only Roarke would help her bridge the gap between then and now, the past and the present. Without his help it was futile to try. Her memory was not coming back, and she was dependent on him.

Martha walked out of the roomlike closet holding a long pale blue sheath in her arms. "This was one of your favorite dresses, Miss Sara, isn't it pretty?"

Sara glanced over her shoulder, then twisted around toward Martha, the eye shadow sponge still held in mid-air. "What a lush color, it is pretty. But why are we getting so dressed up tonight?" She turned back to the mirror again and stroked the sponge across her eyelid.

"When Mr. Roarke came home a few minutes ago, I told him that dinner tonight was going to be very special to celebrate your cast coming off. He said it sounded like a great idea, that he was in the mood for a celebration."

Raising her arms, Sara shimmied her body as Martha slipped the silk over her head and eased it down over her hips. As

Martha zipped it up the back, Sara stared forlornly at her reflection in the full-length mirror. "Oh, Martha, it's beautiful, but it's just too loose. You can sure tell where I've lost my weight." The thin straps held a bodice that gaped a little around her breasts.

Martha pursed her lips, studying the dress, then went back into the closet calling back to Sara, "I know just the thing you need. Ah . . . here it is!"

After Martha left her alone to go downstairs, Sara slowly turned around in front of the mirror, examining herself critically. She had brushed her hair until it lay like spun gold, curled softly on her shoulders, framing her face. Her cheeks were slightly flushed and her eyes sparkled as she studied her reflection. The deep blue of the silk tapestry jacket with its hint of the mysterious orient accented the blue shadow on her eyelids and it covered the loosely fitting bodice of the pale blue sheath beneath. Her amber eyes sparkled yellow in the low light. Somehow she had become caught up with the idea of the celebration and felt excited.

Why am I excited? she mused as she regarded the room. *This is just another dinner with Roarke, nothing more, nothing less.* She slowly limped over to the table in front of the balcony window and admired the crystal vase and candleholders in the center. The room was filled with an air of expectancy, but what was she expecting?

She lit the two tall tapers and watched as the flames flickered to life and twinkled on the crystal. Two perfect roses of deep blood red poised in the crystal vase seemed to flutter under the flames' reflections.

A light tap on the door caused a sharp intake of her breath. The door opened slowly and her heart quivered in her breast. Roarke was so handsome, her mind raced. His blue eyes sparkled when he spied her standing in the glow of the candles. The sheen of his deep burgundy silk shirt strained across the muscular breadth of his chest.

"You look lovely, Sara." He moved smoothly across the room

58

toward her and took her hand in his and lightly kissed the palm. "I have to say, we've celebrated many things, Sara, but this is the first time we've ever celebrated an event of such magnitude. How is your ankle feeling?"

Sara blushed slightly, not from his teasing, but from the touch of his lips on her hand. "It's fine, although I still have to use this"—she pointed to the cane beside her chair—"for a few weeks. But it's great to have a little more mobility." She sat down and motioned for Roarke to join her at the table.

He glanced at the table and the champagne bucket set beside the empty chair. Reaching over, he took the bottle from its icy nest. "When Martha said we were going to celebrate, she really meant it, didn't she?" He pried at the cork and, laughing as it popped, he poured two glasses and handed one to her. Smiling slightly he said, "They're really spoiling you, aren't they? We haven't had champagne since . . ." A disturbed look momentarily flashed in his eyes and he stopped speaking.

Sara had been mesmerized by the touch of his lips on her palm and the low sound of his voice. When Roarke extended his glass toward her, she mentally forced herself to come out of the spell that had been cast. She tapped her glass against his and took a sip of the cold wine, grateful for the chill in her throat because it brought her back to reality. "Martha and Bradley have gone to a lot of trouble, and if they're spoiling me, I love it." She drank some more of the wine and the tingling started to warm her strangely icy body. Baffled, Sara thought, *Why am I so dazed by all of this? Why do I have these surges of anticipation running through me? What am I anticipating anyway?*

Sara looked around her. The room was bathed in a soft golden glow. The only other light in the room besides the candles was the lamp at her bedside. Sara wistfully reflected—if only life could be bathed in a warm golden glow, how nice it would be. The golden warmth smoothed over all the harshness. Candlelight has an effect on people that makes them speak in hushed tones and softens the hard edges of life, the side of life no one

59

wants to admit is there but is reality. Sara shook herself out of her dreaming when she realized Roarke was speaking to her. "I'm sorry, what did you say?" She looked over at him.

"I said, a penny for your thoughts." Roarke leaned back in his chair, his eyes hooded by his long dark lashes.

"I was thinking about candlelight. It makes everything seem so much warmer. Did you ever notice there are no harsh lines in candlelight? Everything is smoothed out and softened." Sara stopped self-consciously. Her candlelight philosophy sounded so absurd when she said it out loud.

Roarke seemed amused. "Candlelight also makes dark corners and some people would be frightened by that. The kind of people who have to have everything right out in the open, with every corner well lit, every secret exposed. Don't dark corners frighten you?" Roarke looked at her intently.

"Dark corners! Roarke, don't you understand my whole life, my whole existence is one large dark corner." Getting up from her chair, Sara grasped her cane and limped over to the balcony window. "I know you find all this hard to believe, but it's true. You think I'm playing some kind of terrible game, but I tell you, I'm not." Sara turned toward the window so he couldn't see the tears that had gathered in her eyes.

Roarke leaped to his feet and stood in front of her. He placed his hands on her shoulders. "Look at me, Sara," he demanded.

She couldn't disregard the command in his voice. Slowly she turned with the faint pressure of his hands and looked deeply into his eyes. Her eyes sparkled in the glow of the candlelight, the unshed tears barely contained, misery echoing in every line of her thin face.

Roarke moved his hand from her shoulder and cradled her face with his palm. "Sara . . ." he groaned. Gently he gathered her into his arms and held her head against his heart. "Sara, I want to believe in you, I want to trust you again."

Sara pulled away and raised her face to look at him. "Why can't you believe in me? What did I do to you to make you doubt me? Please tell me, I have to understand what there was about me that would make you distrust me. Please, Roarke, please! Can't you understand I need to know?" Sara's eyes pleaded with him, her hands gripping his forearms.

Again he moaned her name and gently pulled her to him, his face an anguished mask.

There was a tap on the door and Bradley and Martha came in with their meal. Roarke drew away from Sara and she sagged inwardly, deflated from frustration, wondering what he had been going to do or say. It was the first time since she had come home that he'd been this open with her—open enough at least for her to feel sufficiently safe to expose her fears to him. They went back to the table and sat in silence while Bradley pushed the cart over to them.

Martha busily uncovered dishes and Bradley checked the champagne bottle to see if it needed replacing. Sara could barely control the urge to cry and tried to concentrate on Martha's chatter about the dinner, hoping to divert her stormy thoughts.

Roarke seemed to share her frustration; his movements were abrupt as he lit a cigarette. "Martha, Bradley, thank you for this, however, we will serve ourselves. I'll ring if we should need anything else."

What was his hurry to get rid of them? It didn't matter if they were alone or not. In Sara's mind their moment had been ruined and she despaired of ever having another chance to convince Roarke that he could trust her.

He talked with her about the weather and other trivial matters, but he seemed to be deliberately skirting the subject of the past. Sara became more impatient while listening to his trivial conversation. This was the side of him she had become accustomed to seeing these past weeks. But she didn't want impersonal charm, she wanted honesty.

"Sara, you have to eat more. All you're doing is moving your food around on your plate. You haven't eaten more than a few

61

bites. You'll be back in the hospital if you don't put on some weight soon."

"I just don't have very much of an appetite. Food seems to stick in my throat." Sara threw her napkin on the table. "I think I'll turn on the news." She started to rise from her chair.

Roarke leaned back, watching her intently. "You're doing a lot of things you never did before. Like staring at that TV. You always said television was a waste of time and turned people into mindless zombies." Roarke's cigarette smoke hid his face, and Sara couldn't tell if he was being sarcastic.

She shrunk back in her chair like a balloon that had lost its air. "I've told you a thousand times that I don't know what I did before."

Roarke stubbed out his cigarette and seemed to be in deep thought. A frown creased his handsome forehead and his lips pursed tightly. His face was a closed book; he obviously wanted to keep his thoughts to himself.

CHAPTER FIVE

Roarke poured them more champagne and stood up and prowled around the room sipping his drink. Sara watched him, turning her head as he walked behind her chair. Roarke came back to the table and scooped up the bottle and emptied the remaining champagne into his glass then continued his restless roaming. He picked up the sketch pad lying on the chaise and sat down, setting his glass on the floor beside him. Throwing back the heavy cover, his eyes narrowed as he examined the sketch of his face. Glancing over at Sara, he took the loose page out of the pad and his face clouded when he noticed the second sketch. Tearing the other sheet of paper from the pad, he held the two sketches at arm's length and studied them.

In a low, hoarse rasp, he asked, "When did you do these?" He laid them on the chaise beside him and reached down to pick up his glass.

"This afternoon."

"Both of them?"

"Yes."

Roarke looked over at her, his shadowed face a graphic sculpture of sorrow. "Why are there two?" he said, holding them up again in front of him.

"Well," Sara paused, "I was out on the balcony and had a vivid flashback and when I came out of it, I had drawn one of them."

"And the other?"

"I . . . I did it later," she lowered her head.

He studied them again, absorbed with his thoughts for a few minutes then suddenly he added, "You mean you don't remember doing one of them? Which one?"

She pointed to the drawing of the smiling Roarke in his left hand. "That one."

Again he examined the two sketches. Finally he held up the sketch he clutched in his right hand, the taut, tense face staring back at him. "My God, Sara, is this how you see me? Do I really appear so hard to you?"

Sara got out of her chair, clasped the cane, and went over to stand in front of him. "I don't know what to say, Roarke. I don't want to hurt your feelings but . . . yes, you do. I feel that every time I ask you anything about us, you close yourself off from me. I felt like your prisoner at first and now I'm feeling like your guest, not your wife. I have never felt that you've treated me like your wife, let alone someone who belongs in this house. I've had to put up with it because I don't know what to do or where to go. When I saw what I had drawn at first, I was angry because I don't remember ever seeing you look like that and . . . and in my anger and frustration, I drew that." She pointed to the picture.

Roarke jumped to his feet and threw his arms around her, pulling her roughly to his chest. "My poor Sara, my poor darling. Have I really been that rotten? I've tried to explain to you how confused I am, but I guess I didn't do a very good job of it." His lips touched her forehead. "I'm sorry, Sara." His voice was husky. "I never meant to hurt you so much. I never meant to make you feel like a prisoner. Sara, you don't know how I have to force myself to stay away from your room at night. I stand by your door, listening for any sound, any excuse to come in to you."

"Why haven't you told me this before? Can't you see how much I need you? Haven't I begged you for answers?" She tried to twist out of the steel arms that held her snugly pressed against his broad chest.

"I know you need me, Sara, but I'm not talking about that kind of need. I'm talking about my need to hold you close, to love you. It drives me crazy knowing you're sleeping across the hall, so near yet so far away from me." He lowered his head and brushed his lips across hers.

She jerked her face away. "I know that need, Roarke, I'm very familiar with it. I'm confused by my mixed feelings about you though, my reactions when you touch me. It's like my body remembers you while my mind doesn't. But how can you expect me to give into that instinct when I feel as though you've built a wall between us? You're the one who put me across the hall from you. I didn't."

Roarke tilted her face up. She saw the passion and hurt in his eyes. Her heart picked up its beat and the blood roared in her ears as he said softly, "Let me love you, Sara. Let me show you how I feel, I need you so much."

Roarke pulled her still more tightly against him and Sara hesitantly slid her arms around his waist, lured by his words. Bringing his face close to hers, he placed soft lingering kisses on her cheeks, and Sara could feel her face becoming warm wherever his lips touched her skin. Then his lips tenderly sought hers. He kissed her gently at first but soon hungrily entwined their bodies in a passionate embrace. His lips were soft but firm and tasted sweet. The pressure slowly parted her lips and Roarke's questing tongue invited hers to join his, and as their tongues tentatively touched, she found herself, surprisingly, responding with equal fervor. His hand slipped around and caressed her throat, then she could feel it slide downward to her breasts.

Sara's awakened passion surged through her body. She molded herself to him; the need to have him make love to her overpowered her defenses. Clinging to him, her hands clutching his back, she tried to draw him even closer to her. The familiarity of his kiss, his body, and her response to him shook her to the depth of her soul.

Slowly he moved her jacket off her shoulders and she dropped her arms to let it slide to the floor. Urgently she grasped his body with her hands again, digging her nails into the silky material of his shirt. He kissed the hollow of her throat and ran his tongue along her shoulder. His lips left a trail of fire that ended at her mouth, and his hand slipped the strap of her dress along the soft skin of her upper arm. Stroking her bared breast with his fingertips, he ran kisses down the valley between them and then his lips softly caressed the mounds of silken flesh. Sara didn't want him to stop. She could feel the warmth from his touch rising, slowly, insistently, within her. Her need for him was uppermost in her mind, and she knew her submission to him was absolute.

Roarke's searching lips ceased their exploration and he drew away from her slightly. For one aching moment Sara thought Roarke had decided to blind himself to her needs as he had since she had awakened in the hospital. His eyes questioned hers and she knew her consuming desire to be close to him glowed from her eyes and the answer to his unspoken question was there for him to see. He gently slipped the other strap off her shoulder and his lips lightly touched the skin where the strap had lain, as his hand played with the zipper in the back. The dress slithered down her body and curled around her feet, lying like a blue shadow on the carpet.

"Sara, it's been so long since I've held you," he murmured as he swept her into his arms and carried her over to the bed and lay her down. "Your body is still the silky softness I remember." His fingers tickled over her skin. "Its perfection has haunted me and has made me want you again and again." The tenderness of his touch and his husky voice, filled with desire, held Sara spellbound.

She closed her eyes. She wanted to imprint every word, every sensation into her mind. She needed him, his love, his body, the body that hers remembered. Her need was so strong, it made her tremble. Her body moved sinuously under his touch, rising and falling to the concerto that was being played on her nerves. She felt the warmth of his fingers trace her jawline and earlobes and twine themselves in her long hair. The skin on her body tensed and relaxed, pulsating as the knowing hands and fingers probed and stroked. Slowly she opened her eyes when the sensations that had been bombarding her senses suddenly stopped. Roarke was standing beside the bed removing his clothes and she watched, entranced as his smooth muscular body, a deep bronze in the low lamplight, was revealed.

"Roarke," Sara whispered impatiently through passion-swollen lips. "Touch me, caress me, love me!"

He gazed into her half-closed eyes as he leaned over her, moving closer and closer. Then his mouth sought hers again and his embrace crushed her against him, holding her in a viselike grip. "Sara," he moaned, his lips moving on her lips as he gasped the words, his breath softly mingling with hers. "You're the only woman who could ever make me feel this way. You drive me crazy with desire. I need you so badly." Bare flesh pressed bare flesh, and Sara could feel his burgeoning desire.

As he ran his hands over her, her flesh ignited and inflamed her consciousness. His lips and tongue ran down across her breasts, circling the tip of each and then moved downward across her stomach.

Sara was enthralled, her senses drugged. She was no longer a rational human being. She was nothing but total sensation, a heat that had no fire, a throbbing body with no mind, no reason, just uncontrollable passion. Moaning, and grasping his wavy hair with her hands, the waves of heat rushed through her and her stomach tightened under the force of her tension. Cradling his face with her hands and curving her body, she drew his lips to meet hers. Her voice, guttural with ecstasy, begged, "Roarke, I want you . . . now!"

She clenched her arms around his strong torso and, in her urgency, controlled their tempo. She ascended the fiery peak and, meeting him there, they spiraled down the other side together.

Roarke held her close for a long time and Sara curled languidly against him. For the first time in weeks she felt at peace. Finally she had a sense of belonging. Right now her dark corners held no fear. He kissed the top of her head and lifted her chin, and their eyes met.

If only they could hold on to this afterglow and stay this close. She wondered if these shared emotions could be nurtured and transplanted into their relationship outside the bedroom. If they could, maybe she could find her way to the past and Roarke could trust her again.

Tentatively she reached over and ran her fingertips over his chest, tracing the muscles that glowed in the candlelight, and she played with the dark hairs that covered the sensitive skin. *How could I have forgotten him?*

Roarke leaned over and kissed her forehead then sat up against the headboard. He fumbled around for a cigarette on the tabletop, and when he couldn't find one, got out of bed. He picked up his trousers from the floor where they had been dropped in his earlier haste. Searching in the pockets, he found the pack, lit a cigarette, then sat back down beside her.

Sara sat up, pulling the sheet across her body. "Roarke, was it always this good between us?" she whispered.

The muscled body swung around and Roarke stared at her, his brows meshed together. Taking a deep drag on the cigarette, he said, "Don't you remember? That was the one great thing we shared. You didn't act like you forgot how to make love." He stood up and, with a sharp backward glance, started walking toward the bathroom, gathering his clothes as he went.

Flinging her hand out to him in a pleading gesture, Sara called, "Please, don't walk away! I don't remember!"

Pivoting in his tracks, Roarke stopped short and sneered scathingly, "Well, who have you been practicing with? You sure didn't forget how to please a man!" He reached over and smashed his cigarette into an ashtray.

Sara's hand flew to her mouth. She felt as though he had slapped her. "What . . . what on earth do you mean, who have I been practicing with? Aren't I married to you?" Her eyes glittered then narrowed with anger. "You've been insinuating things ever since I came home. You always seem to bring other men into our conversations. You've made me wonder what kind of a wife I was. Did I cheat on you? Just what in the hell are you talking about?" She wanted to cry. Somehow the spell was broken. Somehow Roarke had managed to crush the tender feelings that had warmed her body.

"How do I know what you've been doing or who you've been doing it with? We haven't lived together for two years!" He froze, clenching his fists by his sides.

Rising to her knees, the sheet falling in a jumble around her hips, she sputtered, "We . . . what?"

Walking toward her, he ground out through gritted teeth, "I didn't want you to know. At least not now and not like this."

Sara reached up and, with balled fists, pounded on his chest, tears streaming down her face. "You bastard," she seethed, "you used me!" He grabbed her fists as she crumpled back down onto the bed. Sobbing, she cried, "That's why I felt like this, like I don't belong. This is why Martha . . . you bastard," she screamed again, "you told Martha and Bradley not to tell me. How could you? You tell me you don't trust me! And you've been lying to me ever since I woke up in the hospital. Pretending you were so happy I was alive." She buried her face in the pillow and with her voice muffled she sobbed, "Oh, why wasn't I killed? Why did I have to live? Go . . . go away, Roarke."

Sitting on the bed, Roarke grabbed her shoulders and, as he turned her to face him, he shook her violently. "Don't ever say that again! I don't ever want to hear you say that again." He pulled her close to him and limply she buried her face in his chest. She just couldn't stand to look at him. "Sara, Sara, I didn't

69

mean to tell you like this, it just slipped out. Believe me, I have my reasons for not telling you about our separation."

Quietly, in a low growl, Sara said, "Why should I believe you? Roarke, let me go. I don't want you to touch me. You used me, and I'll never forgive you for that."

"I needed you and you needed me," Roarke replied coldly, dropping his hands off her shoulders.

"Need? I didn't just need you, I wanted you. My mind might not remember you, but my body hasn't forgotten you." Sara dropped her head to her chest, her long, blond hair falling down across her face like a curtain. "You said you needed me, but not once have you said you wanted me. Do you equate love with sex?"

"Sara, don't be ridiculous. This conversation is getting us nowhere." He got up off the bed, grabbed another cigarette, lit it, and paced around the room. Then, stooping over, he picked up his trousers and put them on, the cigarette tightly clenched in his lips. He walked over to the window and stood with his back to her.

Sara lay back against the piled-up pillows. "Roarke, this is maddening. Tell me about it. You said one of the great things we shared was our bed. What else did we share? Why did we separate?" She saw his shoulders heave with a deep intake of breath.

In a voice so low that Sara had to strain to hear him, he said, "We were happy when we were first married, but as the years went by we seemed to grow apart. Two years ago you packed your bags and moved out. We've been apart ever since. After we separated, you didn't want a divorce, and I agreed. On the night of your accident, when Ted Maxwell called and told me you had been seriously hurt, I went to the hospital and that was the first time I'd seen you in several months." He drew heavily on the cigarette and turned back to her. "Sara, I don't think we should discuss this anymore."

"What do you mean? *You* might not want to discuss it, but

I certainly do. What sort of marriage did we have? Why did we separate? Answer me! Whose fault was it?"

Sara watched him walk across the room and pick up the rest of his clothes. At the bathroom door he paused. "No one's fault and both our fault."

Stunned, she spat, "You are an insensitive brute. So, it's just hit the sack and leave, huh? You got what you wanted. Well, at least you acted like you enjoyed it." She could feel her lips curl in a sneer as she spoke.

Roarke shook his head disgustedly. "In the last few years we were living together, that's about the only thing I did enjoy."

Fury distorted her features. "That's why the marriage failed. That's called lust, not love. How many times did you make me feel used like I do now?" She turned her back on him and buried her head into the pillow again.

To her surprise, she felt a light touch on her arm and heard Roarke's deep voice say softly, "Sara, why do we do this to each other? This was such a wonderful evening. Let's not let it be soured and disintegrate in our fingers. I didn't ever mean for you to feel used. That thought never entered my mind."

Sara hesitantly rolled over to face him, fighting back the tears of anger and hurt. "Did we always fight like this? Is this what you're telling me? I didn't start this tonight, you did. It started out to be such . . . such a beautiful evening. Why do you hate me so much, Roarke? What did I ever do to you?"

"Sara, don't say that! I don't hate you. My God, it's anything but that. I . . ." He looked away from her then spoke again. "Look, I want you to get well, but as I said before, I want you to remember on your own. I'll help you, but I will not discuss our marriage or break-up. Right or wrong, I think your memory should come back automatically without any prodding from me." He took her face between his hands and forced her to look at him. "I'm sorry, I didn't mean for you to feel used. For one beautiful moment the Sara I used to know, the loving, passionate Sara, showed in your eyes, and I forgot you couldn't remember.

71

I was swept away by our passion and it's been so long. Then when you asked me afterward if our lovemaking had always been that good, I guess I was still under your spell and was shocked by your question and thought you were playing games again. You seemed to remember everything . . . everything we liked to share in bed."

"Roarke . . ."

The sound of insistent knocking on the bedroom door interrupted her. Calling out "What is it?," Roarke moved to stand in front of the closed door.

Bradley's voice seeped through the heavy wood. "Sir, I'm sorry to disturb you. You have an urgent call from California. I tried to explain to the party calling that you didn't wish to be disturbed, but they insisted it was very important they speak with you. I was to tell you it concerned some negotiations you're involved in." Bradley sounded upset and embarrassed that he was forced to intrude on their privacy.

"I'll be right there," Roarke replied gruffly. Throwing on his shirt and slipping into his shoes, he said, "Sara, you'll have to excuse me. I'm in the middle of pounding out a contract, and this could be vitally important. We'll continue our conversation some other time. You go to bed now and get some rest, and I'll see you tomorrow." He left her before Sara could utter a word.

She sat as though turned to stone. She couldn't believe he could walk away from her as if they had been having a casual chat. Conversation! This was her life they were talking about!

She didn't have many more answers than she had before. She just had more questions. He kept talking about her game-playing and that he forgot she had amnesia. How could he forget that? What kind of games had she played? Had they really loved each other? Or had they confused lust with love? Why did he want her to remember on her own? He could help her so much and wouldn't. Why had she left him? Was it her fault and he resented it, or was it his fault and he felt guilty?

Then a flush spread through her when she recalled how she

had totally surrendered herself to him, a heat that was new to her but apparently not to the old Sara. The remembrance of her joy and peace after they made love confused her. If she had initiated their separation and if she had left the house willingly, finished with Roarke, why had she given herself now with such abandonment, such unqualified rapture?

Sara stretched out on the bed, rolled over onto her stomach, and propped her chin in the palms of her hands. Her face flushed again as she recalled how her body seemed to know his touch and divine his every wish and desire. Maybe it did appear to Roarke that she remembered, but she knew it was instinct, not memory.

Sara rolled over and stared at the ceiling. She still didn't know how she felt or what to do. Roarke was willing to help her, not as much as she wanted, but at least was willing. And what about the intimate side of their relationship? Tonight the desire that had tried to surface before was fully aroused and satisfied. Did she want to pick up a marriage that had been over for two years and share his bed? Especially when she knew that marriage had left a bitter taste in his mind. Then it hit her! *Is the choice even mine?*

Roarke had again accused her of playing games. Had he decided in his unfathomable mind to play some counter-game to the one he thought she was playing? Her body flushed as she thought of how Roarke's hands had played their melody across her skin. Would he use this as part of his game? She couldn't stand him to humiliate her along with everything else. She dozed as her mind mulled over the new twist her life had taken.

Someone or something was chasing her down an endless tunnel. The blackness enveloped her. The only light she could see was a pinpoint in front of her. As she ran, her hands felt what seemed to be hundreds of doors on either side, but when she grasped the knobs to turn them, they all opened to reveal brick walls. She could sense a presence hovering somewhere in front of her, but when she reached out to grasp for it, she touched

73

nothing but air; the presence had moved somewhere ahead of her. She felt if she could just reach this unknown entity before the thing chasing her could catch her, she would be safe. She was running faster now, but suddenly she felt a hand grab her shoulder and a scream tore raggedly through the black air.

"Sara, Sara! Wake up!"

Roarke's command filtered through her nightmare-laden mind and she realized she was the one who was screaming. Sara thrust her body into a sitting position and opened her eyes. The light on her nightstand was on, and Roarke was sitting on the edge of her bed with his hands gripping her shoulders. Her robe clung to her sweaty body; her hair hung in her eyes and dry sobs wracked her body.

"Oh, Roarke, I had another terrible nightmare. When will they ever stop!" she said with a wrenching moan, and flung herself into his arms.

He smoothed her hair away from her face and rocked her back and forth, trying to calm her. "Shhh, Sara, it's all right now. You're awake and the nightmare's over." His voice washed over her like a lullaby. He kept rocking her back and forth, holding her tightly in his arms. He pressed his lips to her forehead and held her against his heart, waiting for her sobs to ease.

"Don't you understand? Can't I ever make you understand? Whether I'm awake or asleep, my life is a nightmare—one long terrible nightmare. I just can't go on. I can't remember and you won't help me and half the time I don't even think you believe me," she wailed.

"I believe you," he murmured, still trying to calm her.

She jerked away from him. "You don't believe me. You're just saying you do to calm me down. You're humoring me as though I'm crazy." Sara pulled herself out of bed and started limping around the room, wringing her hands, a wild look in her eyes. "Maybe I am crazy. Ted wants me to see a psychiatrist, so that has to be it. That has to be the answer, I'm crazy!" Sobs shook

74

her body. She knew she was almost beyond the point of no return.

Roarke flew across the room and tried to take her into his arms again. "You're not crazy, Sara."

"Don't touch me," she snapped as she wrenched her body out of his grasp. "You don't want me, you won't help me, and I don't even think you like me." Sara ran her hands through her long, dark blond hair, and impotent fury replaced the sobs. She looked like a wild woman, with her hair flung in every direction and her amber eyes narrow slits that shot out sparks of yellow fire mixed with the liquid of her glistening tears.

Roarke grabbed Sara's shoulders and started to shake her. "Sara, snap out of it, pull yourself together." He was practically shouting at her, his face tight from fear, afraid that he would not be able to calm her down.

She blinked her eyes in confusion and stared at him. She didn't attempt to pull away this time.

"Sara, please . . ." He tried to soothe her with a calmer, quieter tone of voice. Roarke guided her across the room to the bed and they both sat down facing each other. "You know what you've said isn't true. You're upset because of this nightmare." He gently pushed back the matted hair laying on her cheek. "You said this was another nightmare. Have you had others?"

Sara slowly nodded her head, wiping the back of her hand across her eyes.

"Why haven't you told me you were having nightmares?"

She dropped her hands into her lap, bowing her head to stare at her fidgeting fingers. "I didn't tell you about the dreams because I didn't think you'd be interested."

Roarke gave her a bewildered look and put his hand over hers. "I could use a cup of coffee. How about you? Will you be okay while I'm downstairs?"

Sara looked at him blankly and nodded her head. "I'll be fine," she whispered.

When she was alone, Sara was almost too numb to think. She

got up from the bed and stumbled into the bathroom, rinsed her face with cold water, then lethargically walked back into the bedroom and sagged down on the bed like someone in a trance.

Her insides were writhing and she could feel every nerve throbbing throughout her body. *I can't stand anymore tonight, I just can't stand it,* she fretted. Exhaustion weighed heavy on her. She felt that it was a massive effort to take one breath after another.

I just hope he doesn't start on me again. I'd probably curl up in a ball and fade away if he did. She shivered with the thought.

Roarke came back carrying a tray that held two steaming mugs. He set the tray on the table and carried the mugs over and sat down on the bed beside Sara. "Martha heard me rattling around in the kitchen and insisted on making hot chocolate for us."

Sipping the hot, spicy liquid, some life seemed slowly to ebb back into Sara's spiritless body. She was still feeling somewhat confused, but the hysteria she had felt earlier seemed to be dwindling away.

"Are you feeling any better?" Roarke asked. "Do you feel like talking?"

"I don't know. Are we going to have another conversation?" she asked in a snide tone of voice. "If we are, then forget it."

"What the hell is that supposed to mean?"

Laughing bitterly, she answered, "You said earlier that we'd continue our *conversation* later. Is this later? My life is one big mess, most of which I don't remember, and you act like it's just another topic for a casual conversation. You should have brought us a cup of tea, isn't that what ladies drink? You know, tea and conversation."

"What the hell has gotten into you?" Roarke shook his head. "Sara, why is it you take everything I say the wrong way? No matter what I say or do I feel I'm wrong." His voice cracked and he put the mug to his lips. His black hair fell over his forehead and the lines around his mouth looked deep and dark.

Spontaneously Sara's hand went out and she touched his cheek. He was as vulnerable as she was. "Roarke, I don't do it on purpose. One minute you seem to care and are compassionate, and the next you're putting that damned wall between us. You keep me off-balance all the time. When you say something, I never know whether you're being sarcastic or whether you really mean it. I don't know how to think or how to act anymore. I don't know what to do . . . I just don't know."

His eyes bored into hers. "I don't know what to think either. But you shouldn't take everything I say and twist it until I don't recognize that I've said it or even know why I said it. Please, just trust me that I know what's best for us." His eyes begged her as his hand crept up and held hers tightly against his cheek.

Sara looked into his face, searching for what she thought she heard in his voice and her breath caught in her throat. The man sitting beside her was the Roarke that she had sketched during her flashback. His eyes were warm and soft and his mouth was curved with a smile of compassion. Somewhere inside her something began to melt and her heart started to swell. The emotion flowed through her body until her fingers tingled. She realized with a shock that it was love that flowed through her withered heart and filled her with warmth. She loved Roarke! She shook her head in disbelief. She loved this man, this enigma.

Quietly, so as to not let him know the turn her mind had taken, she said, "If you really think you know what's best for us, then I'll go along with you, because I sure don't know. I'm willing to trust you. Don't ask me why, but I am. But one thing you have to understand is that my life is like a nightmare. It's like living with only your sense of touch alive and burning yourself everywhere you turn!" Sara put her cup down on the nightstand and turned back to Roarke. "I said I'm willing to try to trust you. But are you willing to trust me? If you'll think back, you know there were times you doubted that I have amnesia. And sometimes I feel like the only emotion you feel for me is pity."

"I don't pity you, Sara." Roarke's eyes had a sincerity she

77

couldn't doubt. "Maybe the trouble has been me, pitying myself. I have had my doubts that you have amnesia, especially on the day you were to come home from the hospital and I saw Ted Maxwell, kneeling at your feet, holding you. I thought you were playing another game. I thought Ted was another spider you wanted to attract into your web," Roarke said flatly, his eyes never moving from Sara's face.

Sara listened to him intently. She didn't like what she was hearing. She got up and went over to the window. She felt she needed some space between them if she were going to objectively absorb what he was telling her. "Good grief, what kind of a person was I? Obviously I was really a witch or you'd never have jumped to that conclusion. A spider spinning webs! Is that what you think of me?" Sara put her hand up to rub her temple and turned to face Roarke. "Won't you change your mind and start at the beginning and tell me everything? Tell me every last detail," she said with an edge of sorrow to her voice.

"What good would it do to go through every detail?" he asked. "You'll remember it quickly enough. I want to trust you again, so let's start trusting each other from now on." He walked over to her and stood facing her but made no attempt to touch her. "If you have a question when you remember something, we'll talk about it, honestly and openly."

"But what about us? What about the past and your feelings about it?" she questioned him.

"This is our beginning, Sara. Let's begin as friends. Friends who believe in and trust each other." He took her hands into his. "We won't rush or push it. I think you're a new person and maybe I can become a new person through you." At her questioning expression he explained. "You used to question my every move; you didn't trust me at all. Now you seem to want to trust me and believe in me. That's the foundation we'll build on." He took her face between his hands and kissed her lightly on the lips. "I think it's time you went to sleep now, you've got dark circles under your eyes." He smiled tenderly down at her while he traced the dark smudges with his finger.

Roarke steered Sara toward the bed and made sure she was under the covers before he turned out the bedside light. "I'm going to leave your door open and mine also. If you need me for anything, just call."

"Roarke," Sara called out to his retreating back.

He turned in the doorway. "Yes?" He looked at Sara huddling under the covers. The light from the hall shone on her hair that spread over the pillow, making her look young and vulnerable.

"Someday I'll have to know about our past. I can't go through life with blinders on."

"You'll remember it all soon enough, and maybe by then we'll have found out what we're both really like and the past won't matter so much. We'll make our present so strong, the past will seem like a dream," he stated positively.

"More like a nightmare, don't you mean?" she asked pensively.

"No more talk about nightmares. I'll see you in the morning," he ordered. "Good night."

Sitting up, she implored, "Roarke, just one more thing. What about the marriage? After all, you said we've been separated for two years. A lot of things must be changed in your life. Maybe a wife doesn't fit in anymore, even a wife who's just a friend. I don't want you to feel obligated to resume a marriage you no longer want."

Roarke turned to face her again. The light was behind him and all that Sara could see of Roarke was a black silhouette in the doorway. "Sara, a lot has changed in my life. I found out I don't like being alone. That kind of life doesn't appeal to me at all. And after this evening, I realize that I need you in my life. I don't have any answers about our future. For now, let's live in the present. Good night, Sara," he said once again and went into the hall, leaving the door open several inches.

Sara tried to settle down, but sleep eluded her. Roarke had

said he was willing to begin again. And even if she couldn't remember the past, she knew that right now, this minute, she loved Roarke. She was never more sure of anything in her topsy-turvy world. If he wanted to build a foundation of trust and friendship, she would cement the foundation with love.

She couldn't remember, but she was absolutely sure she had loved Roarke all along. Not knowing why they separated or anything about the marriage didn't make any difference. Her love felt right, it felt good, it was familiar to her.

Roarke hadn't spoken of love tonight and maybe he never would. She knew she couldn't let him know that she loved him; it might make him regret his decision to try again. Sara didn't want that to happen, not only because she needed him, but because she wanted him near her. She wanted to talk and get to know this man her heart and body already loved.

He hadn't said if there was another woman in his life. Maybe he was trying to imply there might be another woman when he said he didn't like being alone. He was a handsome man and very virile. Surely he hadn't spent the last two years celebate. But was there anyone special in his life—a woman who had become important to him, a woman who had eased his lonely hours, a woman who didn't play the games he accused her of playing?

Sara turned over and pounded her pillow. All these negative thoughts were getting her nowhere. He had said he needed her in his life even if it were just as a friend. Well, maybe she could become more to him. They had been in love once, and it could happen again. Could she hope to rekindle a flame that might be dead, or should she? She didn't have an answer, but at least the door wasn't closed anymore.

CHAPTER SIX

Slowly Sara descended the stairs, her slippers quiet on the heavy carpet. She gazed around in amazement. When Roarke had brought her here weeks ago, she hadn't had time to really see anything. "It's lovely," she whispered, awed by the serene beauty of the foyer. The wide, open arch on the left revealed the living room, and she regarded the elegant furnishings for a few minutes. She could partially see the dining room through another arch at the end of the living room, its massive crystal chandelier sparkling in the sunlight, tossing prisms of color on the cool white walls.

She noticed two doors on the other side of the entry. One was closed, but the other was slightly ajar. Peering into the slight opening, she pushed the door open and recognized the room from Martha's description. This had to be her den, she thought. Paintings, paints, and easels were stacked against the one wall, and an easel was standing in the corner just as Martha had told her.

She went over to the easel and examined the canvas that was propped on its crossbar. The firm material was covered with a pale wash of colors. She reached out and touched it. *How did I know it's called a wash?* she wondered as she ran her hand over the resilient canvas. Turning around, she scanned the entire room. It wasn't large, but was bright with the light coming through the wall of windows. The only furniture was a love seat, a small table, and one chair. There were books on a row of shelves against the wall by the door—books about painters, museums, galleries. Paintings hung on the third wall—a profusion of paintings with no rhyme or reason, a riot of color and subjects. When she moved closer, she realized they all had a single name on them, just Alexander, no first name. But she knew they were hers.

Moving over to the stack of canvases that leaned against the first wall, she bent over and sorted through them, glancing at each one quickly. Then she stopped abruptly and pulled one out and placed it in front of the stack. She backed up to the love seat and sat down and studied it in rapt concentration. It was the finished painting she had seen herself sketching in her flashback. It was Roarke sitting on the beach, his hair ruffled by the ocean breeze, the sand, tall grass, ocean, and sky surrounding him, making him an integral part of the scene. It was bold and exciting, just like Roarke.

Leaning back, she looked around her in wonder. Even though so much of herself was missing, she somehow knew she was good: She had talent. It was a part of her, a part that hadn't disappeared with the accident or her memory loss. It was as instinctive as breathing, writing, talking, and loving Roarke. She was impatient to pick up a brush and paint. Maybe through her painting and her loving she could find all the missing pieces and put herself back together.

She picked up a sketch pad that lay on top of the table, opened it, and saw a drawing of a garden and an old woman in a floppy straw hat stooped over, digging in the earth around some bushes. She tore it out of the pad and, as she stared at the bent-over figure, she picked up a pencil and began sketching a face on the tablet.

The lines of the face began to take form and shape. The eyes were lively but held a hint of pain, or was it sadness? The mouth was small, but its smile filled the face. Wrinkles were a cross-stitch over the skin, but they added character to the features. The hair was brushed back severely away from the broad forehead and caught in a large chignon at the nape.

Sara laid the pencil down; it was the face of the old woman she had dreamed about, and the face was still a vivid imprint on her mind.

"I wondered where you had gone!"

Sara's head shot up, startled by the voice that had intruded on her brooding.

"I went up to see if you wanted some lunch, and I couldn't find you." Martha sat down beside Sara. "I'm glad you finally decided to leave that room."

"Well, I've had a couple days to practice walking around my room without the cast. I've walked with and without the cane and my ankle feels almost as good as new. I decided to venture out today and see what the rest of the house looks like."

"Mr. Roarke will be so glad to hear this when he comes home today. Before he left for California the other day, he asked me to try and coax you out of your room."

"Yes, I guess he will be pleased," Sara murmured, wondering if this three-day separation had given Roarke time to think over and regret his decision for them to try again. She had had second and third thoughts about their evening and everything they had said to each other, but she hadn't changed her mind. She loved him and something inside her was obsessed with trying to win him back. When he had come to her room the morning after her nightmare and told her that he had to leave immediately for California, he had seemed pensive and frustrated at having to go. He had even told her he'd miss her and she hoped he would because she missed him.

"Miss Sara, what's wrong?"

Flustered, not wanting to tell Martha what she was thinking, she glanced down at the sketch pad on her lap. She handed the sketch to Martha. "Martha, who is she?"

Martha looked at the sketch, then at Sara, a sad expression

passing quickly across her face. "It's your grandmother. Did you just draw this?"

Sara nodded absently, trying to fit this new piece into her puzzle.

"What brought this face to your mind? Did you remember something?"

"No, I didn't really remember. I had a dream last night, or rather early this morning."

"Do you want to tell me about it?" the older woman asked quietly.

"Well, in my dream, I was somewhere that was foggy and the air was damp. The ground felt spongy and tried to clutch at my shoes when I walked on it. There were huge marble stones, and they seemed to surround me on all sides." Sara shuddered. "It wasn't until I saw two coffins that I realized I was in a cemetery. The coffins were sitting on the misty ground, covered with flowers and lots of people were standing around, some of them crying. I—I didn't recognize any of the faces except an old lady who was holding my hand tightly. I felt as though I knew her. We were dressed in black and crying. When I jolted awake, I imagined I could still feel the woman's hand holding mine."

Martha remained silent throughout Sara's recollection, but the expression on her face alarmed Sara. "What's the matter, Martha, why do you look so disturbed? Have I said something to upset you? What is it?" Sara touched Martha's cheek with the palm of her hand.

Martha took Sara's hand and pressed it warmly between hers. "I'm upset because it makes my heart break that in order for you to become a whole person again, you have to remember the tragedies of your life along with the happy things. What a shame that you can't be allowed to remember only the good."

Sara smiled poignantly and her heart lurched. She realized how much Martha did love her. It was as though she were Martha's own daughter.

Martha sighed. "The dream you had really happened. The

84

older woman who held your hand so lovingly was your grandmother. Your parents were both killed in a horrible head-on collision one night on their way home from a party. A drunk driver who was passing a truck . . . they were killed instantly." Martha broke off with a shake of her head.

Sara was trembling, partly from the horror of her parents' untimely and horrible deaths and partly from the excitement of her remembering something of the past, even if it were in a dream. "Do we have any photographs of my parents or grandmother?" she asked breathlessly, hoping against hope that the answer would be yes. She was elated when Martha told her there was an album upstairs and could hardly contain herself until they got to her room and Martha brought the album to her.

The woman in her dream and in her sketch was indeed her grandmother. The pictures of her parents saddened her but brought no memory other than the feeling of sorrow. But Sara was more optimistic than she had been in the last several weeks. If she could remember the funeral and her grandmother, maybe soon she'd remember the rest.

Martha's voice invaded Sara's thoughts. "Miss Sara, do you want some lunch now? I have to get started on dinner soon. Why don't you come back downstairs and eat it in the kitchen and we'll talk while you eat." She clapped her hands together and a smile split her face. "I know, why don't you and Mr. Roarke eat in the dining room tonight? We'll celebrate you first day out of your room and Mr. Roarke's homecoming!"

"Two celebration dinners in one week?" Sara laughed. "It sounds to me that you look for any excuse to cook a big meal and fuss over us."

Sara spent a great deal of time on herself in anticipation of dinner with Roarke. After her shower she brushed her hair till it shone like golden silk around her face and shoulders. She chose a pastel pink, full-length dress and pink shoes to match. The dress flowed against her body, molding her lovely, lithe form, the

85

bodice draped over her breasts, clinging softly to the round firmness underneath. She wore very little makeup, but her eyes glowed and her cheeks flushed with expectation.

"Sara, you never looked lovelier," a deep voice sounded from the open doorway. Roarke leaned against the door frame, his suit jacket flung casually over his shoulder and his hair a trifle rumpled.

Sara hadn't heard her door open but was pleased when she turned and saw him. "Thank you, kind sir," she quipped with a slight dip of her head in a mock curtsy.

"You're dazzling and Martha is bustling around the kitchen and Bradley is hovering near the dining room. Is this all for me?" He smiled as he took her hands in his, his blue eyes filled with sparks of light.

"Yes, it's our way of saying welcome home to you. We missed you." Sara smiled into his eyes. "And we're eating dinner in the dining room tonight. We're also celebrating my first evening downstairs."

"Well, maybe I should go away more often. It's quite clear that absence does make the heart grow fonder," he teased.

"How did your trip go? Is everything taken care of?" Sara frowned. She wanted to share in his life, but she didn't know enough about his business to ask intelligent questions.

"It went really well. Not only will we make a considerable profit, but there are some long-range benefits, including more prestige for the firm. I'd better go shower and change clothes before Martha skins me alive for being late and ruining her dinner. If you wait for me, I'll walk you downstairs," he offered. "It will only take me a few minutes."

"I'll wait for you. I still have a few things to do myself." She smiled.

"Okay, I'll be back to get you in less than fifteen minutes."

Sara watched him until he was in his room and behind the closed door. She clasped her hands across her stomach. It was churning from the excitement of having him home again, from having him close. She yearned to tell him about her discovery of her love for him, but knew she couldn't. She hoped that soon she could tell him how much she cared.

Twenty minutes later they were seated in the dining room with Bradley serving them. He poured their wine and Sara proposed a toast. "Here's to the success you've had with this contract, may you have much more success in the future." She held her glass in mid-air, waiting for Roarke to tap his against it.

"Here's to you, Sara. A beautiful woman who is once again stealing her husband's heart!" Roarke looked tenderly into her eyes as he touched his glass to hers.

Sara wanted to run over and throw herself into his arms and entice him upstairs to her bedroom. But she knew she had to move slowly. There was a lot of hurt in both of them to overcome.

Throughout dinner Roarke regaled her with stories of when their house was new, how they scoured the countryside for a particular piece of furniture that Sara wanted.

In Roarke's study after dinner they drank coffee and continued their light conversation. Roarke was charming and amusing and Sara was entranced. She watched his blue eyes change color as he would swing emotionally from telling her something funny to something poignant. His face dropped the mask of guarded defensiveness, and the play of reactions that softened his features was fascinating.

Contemplating his magnificent handsomeness, Sara thought to herself, *Wouldn't we make beautiful children?* Without thinking she blurted out, "Roarke, why didn't we have any children?" With a gasp Sara put her hand over her mouth, regretting the impulsively asked question. The shuttered look that came over Roarke's face told her she had ventured too far too fast.

Deciding since she had gone this far she might as well pursue the subject despite Roarke's change of mood, she added, "You said you'd be honest with me and answer my questions. Don't shut me out, Roarke, please."

Roarke stood up and walked over to the bar, his shoulders slumped. He poured himself a drink from a crystal decanter and kept his face averted. Finally, in a toneless voice, he answered, "We had wanted children. We wanted to start a family right away, but after the honeymoon we decided we should wait for a year or two and have some time to ourselves. I thought it was a good idea. You were very young and I was young enough where a little time wouldn't hurt. Later you decided that one more year wouldn't hurt, and it just went on that way until we separated. I never questioned our decision because I felt you needed time to mature. In later years I realized our marriage was in trouble and to bring a child into a marriage that was going bad wasn't fair to the child." He pulled out a cigarette and after lighting it poured himself another drink.

Sara stared at her hands, deep in thought. This other woman Roarke talked about seemed totally disassociated from her. It was as though there were two Saras, and the more Sara heard about the other one, the less she liked her. She cringed inwardly when she saw the hurt in Roarke's eyes and the tension in his body over the havoc the other Sara had created in his life. When he spoke of the other one, she winced with shame, embarrassment, and deep hurt that she really was the person who could cause this change in him. She felt like a mirror, with the horrible Sara on one side of the mirror constantly reflecting through to the side Sara was on now.

"I don't . . . I don't have any defense or explanation because I don't know this person you're talking about. It's like we're talking about a stranger, a stranger who haunts this house," Sara said regretfully. She got up to leave the room, feeling she had spoiled their wonderful evening, but until her memory returned, she knew this would happen often.

"Sara, please don't leave. I didn't mean to be so short with you. You're right when you say ghosts haunt this house. But I think they're ghosts we can put to rest. Come over here and let's sit down a minute."

If only they could put the ghosts to rest, but how? She sat down beside him and he looked deeply into her eyes.

"Roarke, I'm sorry if I upset you," Sara said quietly, "but regardless of what you think, there are many things I need to know. Do you realize how alone and frightened I am? My nightmares are becoming more frequent. The horrible part is that even when I dream of the past, I really don't remember it. One thing I do know though—I don't like the other Sara. She's the ghost who haunts this house." Sara felt her agitation increasing, but she couldn't stop herself. "I'm so afraid that when I do get my memory back, I'll be the old Sara, and I don't want to be her! The more I hear of her, the less I like her. I have such a helpless feeling. I'm afraid that I can't stop her from coming back."

Roarke's forehead was creased with worry. "Sara, try not to be so frightened. That's not going to help. Listen"—he smiled and chucked her under the chin with his fingertips—"you weren't all bad. My God, if you would have been, I wouldn't have married you. We had a lot of good times together."

"But I couldn't defend myself even if you did tell me now what had gone wrong or some of the things I did to you. I don't remember what I did or why I did them."

"I wouldn't tell you anyway, Sara," Roarke interjected. "There would be no use in going over who is to blame. I told you before, we're both at fault. What is past is past and what matters is right now. We're both different people, so we'll take each day as it happens and each other as we are now." Roarke smiled again, his face relaxing, and he reached over and took her hands that she was twisting together in her lap, held them in his, and rubbed them. "I am beginning to believe that you're not the same woman who haunts us from the past. I'm almost positive that woman no longer exists." He kissed the wrists of both her hands. "I want to know the new you. We'll find a way to bridge the gap between our past and the present."

The contact of Roarke's lips on the thin flesh of her wrists was like an electrical shock. Sitting very still, she tried to keep her voice low and even. "Roarke, I honestly don't know what to say. Starting a new beginning is very easy for me because this is my beginning. But this can't be easy for you, I know that. I can't even begin to imagine all the hurt we've been through, but I sometimes can see the pain in your eyes. Are you sure this is what you want to do and not something you feel obligated to do?" She reached out and put her hand on his shoulder. His flesh under his silky shirt was warm and firm beneath her hand.

"Sara, if I weren't sure, I wouldn't be sitting here now. Of course I'm sure. You are fascinating, warm, and understanding, and I want to know you better." Roarke reached up and took her hand from his shoulder and kissed the palm. "And you aren't alone. You have Martha, Bradley, and me. We all care about you."

Sara blinked back tears that were forming in her eyes. "I know that, but what about my friends, our friends? We do have some friends, don't we? No one has called or come to visit me. Are they afraid of me? Do they think amnesia is a contagious disease or a form of insanity?"

Roarke put his fingers over her lips to stop the words. "I thought we settled that a good while ago. You're not crazy. I don't want to hear another word about that! Our friends have called, and I asked them all to have patience until you're well. We thought you had enough to contend with in getting over your accident. And Ted said with your amnesia you could do without a lot of confusing people hanging around."

Leaning her head back against the sofa, Sara sighed audibly and closed her eyes. Roarke squeezed her hands and she opened her eyes again and looked at him.

"Listen, Sara, we can't keep dwelling on this. We've sat here most of the evening talking about a new beginning, but we can't start if we keep rehashing the past. This started out as an evening we both looked forward to. We've had our serious talk. Now let's get on with the fun part."

Sara also desperately wanted to recapture the gay mood of

earlier in the evening. She had looked forward to Roarke's homecoming with such anticipation and apparently so had he. His charming conversation at dinner and his concern for her well being made her feel so wanted. She didn't want to constantly be complaining or worrying. He certainly wouldn't look forward to coming home if she were that kind of woman.

"But, Roarke"—Sara looked up at him mischievously—"I—I don't remember how to have fun either!" Mirth bubbled up inside her and she couldn't contain it. Her eyes were shining and the sound of her giggling filled the room.

Roarke threw his head back and laughed. It was the first time Sara had heard him laugh aloud in the weeks that she had been with him. His laughter was deep and filled with vibrant warmth. This is how she wanted to see him all the time—his eyes twinkling, a smile lighting up his face, and his deep laughter warming the room.

"You're a nut, a cute one, but still a nut." He tweaked the end of her nose with his fingers. "Well, as I recall, you used to be a fanatical gin player. Would you like to play cards?"

"I guess, but you'll . . ." Sara chuckled.

"What's so funny?" he asked with one eyebrow raised.

"I was about to say again, you'll have to refresh my memory—" Sara's words caught on a sob that suddenly came out of nowhere.

Roarke was beside her instantly. "Don't cry, Sara!" he said, taking her into his arms and caressing her back. He looked at her with a strange glint in his eye. "You weren't that bad at playing gin." He gasped as Sara grinned and pretended to hit him.

Sara grabbed one of the throw pillows she had been leaning against and hit him on the head with it. "So, I'm a bad gin player, huh? Get out the cards and let's see who's a bad gin player."

Roarke retreated from the barrage of throw pillows that were aimed in his direction. Sara sat back and sighed a deep sigh of contentment. Maybe they had salvaged the evening.

Roarke walked back to the sofa and moved the things around

on the coffee table so they would have room to play cards. He sat down and shuffled the deck, the cards a blurred flurry of cardboard in his hands.

Sara sat up straight and pretended to roll up her sleeves. "Okay, deal! Just give me the details, then be prepared to lose." Roarke laughed and Sara almost dropped the cards out of her hand. She gazed at him, and his smiling face made her breathless. Her love for him nearly overwhelmed her senses. She loved him so much, could she be the kind of woman he could love? How she wanted to be, she wanted to be everything to him—his friend, his companion, his wife and, most of all, she wanted to be his lover. Shaking her head, she tried to concentrate on what Roarke was telling her about the play of the cards. Telling him she thought she understood, they started the game.

After a few minutes Sara drew a card from the pile in the middle of the table, placed it among those in her hand, put the cards face up on the table, and called, "Gin!" She laughed at Roarke's amazed expression.

Later Roarke threw his cards down. "You sure didn't forget how to play gin, did you? I've been losing consistently for the past hour."

"Well, there are just some things a girl never forgets," Sara quipped. "I guess I'm a natural-born gambler. But don't think you are going to get away that easily, with just a compliment. We were playing for money, remember?" she said with mock sternness. "There's still some accounting to do. Let me see . . ." Sara picked up the tablet laying beside Roarke. "That's exactly five hundred dollars you owe me, sir. Pay up!" Sara put the tablet down and held out her hand in demand for payment.

Roarke stood up and felt his pockets then pulled them inside out. "All I have is thirty cents and my key chain. Will that do?"

Teasingly Sara chided him. "Don't you know you shouldn't gamble unless you can afford it?"

"Oh, I can pay, ma'am, if you'll just step over here." With a beckoning finger, he pointed to the place where he stood.

"There's all kinds of payment. Maybe we could use the barter system. I'll trade a kiss for what I owe you."

Sara slowly rose from the sofa and went over to him. "That's an expensive exchange, don't you think? A kiss for five hundred dollars? I guess I'll have to be the judge to see if it's worth it."

He grasped her and roughly tipped her back into the cradle of his arms. He stared down at her greedily. "There are just some kisses that are worth more than others, ma'am." He pretended to ruffle her hair, then a gentleness overcame both of them. He kissed her throat and then, lavishing her face with a loving gaze, he lowered his lips and kissed her mouth. They stood, bodies locked together in a kiss that deepened. Sara slid her arms around him and pulled her body closer to his. As she felt his fingers coil in her hair and his kiss consume her, the floodgate of her desire burst open.

"Roarke . . . oh, I'm sorry, I hope I'm not interrupting anything."

Roarke and Sara parted abruptly. Startled, they turned as one toward the voice that had interrupted their embrace. Sara's eyes were still misty from her passion, and it took her several seconds to focus on the woman who was standing in the doorway.

"Suzanne, what the hell are you doing here?" Roarke moved away from Sara, walked over to the coffee table, and reached for his cigarettes.

Ignoring his question, the woman flung open her arms and rushed toward Sara. "Sara, darling, how good to see you."

Sara stood as still as a statue, watching the strange woman move toward her. Who was she? Then the woman's arms went around her, and Sara flinched as she endured a quick kiss on her cheek.

Stepping back, the woman gushed, "Sara, I've wanted to come to see you long before this, but your mean husband wouldn't let me. You poor dear, you've been through so much and then for Roarke not to allow you to see your old friends is just more than I can understand."

Bewilderedly turning to Roarke for help, Sara saw him turn his back and walk over to the bar. "Do you want a drink, Sara?" He paused slightly then added, "Suzanne?"

"Yes, darling, please. I've been at a beastly boring party and I just decided on a whim to barge in here and say hello."

Sara forced herself to move and collapsed on the couch. Who was this person? She cleared her throat and said, "Roarke, I'd like some brandy, please." When he brought it to her, she looked at him quizzically.

He blinked as awareness swept over his face. "I'm sorry, Sara. I guess I forgot again. This is Suzanne Morrison."

"Oh, Roarke." Suzanne swirled her glass, the ice making a tinkling sound as the cubes chased each other around the sides of the glass. "I forgot she wouldn't remember me. Isn't it a shame, she's been through so much, hasn't she? Roarke, do tell her who I am."

Sara turned to the stunning woman and in a soft, controlled voice said, "I'm not deaf, Miss Morrison, I just have amnesia. You don't have to act as though I'm an invalid or incompetent. You can talk to me. I am here."

"Oh, Sara, I am sorry. I guess I was being rude." The green eyes glittered. "I don't know how to handle this, I'm sorry. I've known you for years, Sara. Please call me Suzanne. It sounds so strange for you to call me by my last name. The four of us were friends, you and Roarke and Bob and myself."

"Bob?" Sara asked.

"My . . . late husband." She took a quick sip of her drink.

Sara studied the svelte figure in green. Suzanne was taller than she was, and with the high-heeled shoes she wore, she was almost as tall as Roarke. Her black hair was caught up in a Gibson girl style and little ringlets of hair were left to cling at her temples and nape. She wore a deep emerald green dress. The skirt was split up the side to her thigh and the bodice plunged to her waist in the front. Sara marveled at how small the pieces of material

94

were that covered her voluptuous body. The neckline showed off her cleavage and the rounded swell of half her breasts.

Sara felt a twinge of envy. Most anyone else wearing such a gown would look vulgar, but Suzanne looked sensuous and stunning. Her makeup was done to perfection, and her green eyes were heavy-lidded and soft and the phrase "bedroom eyes" came into Sara's mind. Her nose was narrow and tipped up at the end and her mouth was the same red as her nail polish, with a full pouty bottom lip. She was definitely beautiful, but she had an aura about her of a panther on the prowl. Sara shivered at the thought.

"Look, Sara," Suzanne said, "I want to know all about how you're doing. When are you going to be able to get out? We'll have to have lunch downtown and celebrate your recovery. Is there anything I can do to help you?"

"I'm fine and lunch sounds like a nice idea. But right now I can't think of anything you could do for me," Sara replied guardedly, not looking at Suzanne but at Roarke for some kind of help, some answers. But he wouldn't meet her eyes. She was curious about his seeming discomfort and reticence to look at her.

Suzanne turned back and concentrated her attention on Roarke. "Roarke, the Robinsons are going to meet me in an hour at the Bolling air force base officer's club. General Robinson is quite anxious to talk with you. He wants to discuss that government contract with you, that nice big one you're interested in," she murmured softly, putting her free hand on Roarke's arm with a fluttering motion.

Roarke moved away from her and sat down in the chair opposite the sofa, turning his body slightly to face the fireplace.

Suzanne moved over to Sara and sat on the couch beside her. "Look, Sara, we've been friends for a long time. This meeting with General Robinson has been so hard to set up. Do you mind if I steal Roarke away from you for an hour or so? It's really important for him to meet with the general. I tried to call Roarke at the office today to tell him I had finally arranged this and left several messages, but he never returned my calls."

Roarke stiffened slightly in his chair. "I didn't go to the office. I came straight home from the airport."

"Well, that explains it. Honestly, Roarke, there are times when you're absolutely impossible to get in touch with. Were you two playing some new game I haven't heard of?" Suzanne asked, pointing to Roarke's pockets that were still turned inside out.

Roarke looked over at Suzanne with a frown on his face. "We were playing gin. Sara beat me and won some money. I was just showing her that I didn't have any money on me . . . oh, never mind. Sara, do you mind if I go along with Suzanne to see General Robinson? She's right, he's so damned busy running around the world and I'd like to get a handle on this contract."

Sara stood, trying to keep a tight rein on her befuddlement. "I—I don't mind if it's important. If you'll excuse me, I'm tired. I think I'll go to my room." Sara couldn't look at either of them. She just turned, her head held high, and walked to the door. Her eyes were filled with tears of hurt ready to spill over her lashes.

Roarke was suddenly behind her with his hand on her elbow. "I'll walk with you to your room."

"Good night Sara, I hope to see you soon. I'll call you tomorrow. I'll bring Roarke back safe and sound, I promise."

Sara's back stiffened. "Good night, Suzanne" was all she could manage to say and she could barely choke that out. Once they were in the foyer by the stairway Sara turned to Roarke. "I can walk to my room without any help. Please don't leave Suzanne on my account. Good night." She spun around and walked up the stairs as fast as she could and still maintain some dignity.

"I'll see you later, Sara." Roarke's voice floated after her up the stairway.

Sara turned to face him. For the first time since Suzanne's appearance, his eyes met and held hers. All she could do was stare down at him. Her hurt must have clearly shown in her eyes.

I don't care if he does know I'm hurt, Sara thought to herself. *After all, he could have told her no, that he'd make other arrangements to see that general.*

Roarke started up the stairs toward her. "Sara . . ."

"Roarke, could you hurry a little? After all, it is quite a drive to Bolling." Suzanne stood at the doorway of the study, one hand on her hip and the other almost caressing the door frame.

Sara turned and continued her way up to her room, not caring to hear or see any more of the scenario at the foot of the steps. She closed and locked the door of her bedroom behind her. Leaning against the barrier placed between Roarke and herself, she let the tears she had been holding back flow down her cheeks.

She heard Roarke's soft tapping on her door, and when it became clear she was not going to answer him, the muffled sounds of his voice sifted into her room. But she still didn't open the door and in a few moments she heard him leave.

Sara threw herself across the bed and wept. How could this happen? How could he have agreed to meet these people with Suzanne just when they were having such a wonderful evening? Their relationship was growing, a thread linking them together in the present and hopefully to their past. But maybe she was fooling herself, maybe there was no way to link the past to the present. Maybe this is why she had left him, that his business came first and he didn't care who he used or who he hurt.

CHAPTER SEVEN

Sara blinked her eyes at the early morning sunlight streaming through the window. She rubbed them, trying to relieve the heavy, gritty feeling from too much crying and too little sleep. What fitful sleep she did get had been filled with terrible nightmares. More than once during the night she jerked awake with her heart pounding and her face damp with perspiration. This morning she couldn't remember any of the dreams, just vague subconscious feelings and fatigue as evidence that they had occurred.

She stumbled over to the balcony door, pulled it open, and went outside to let the fresh late spring air sweep the cobwebs from her brain. She needed to think, but her brain was fuzzy and she couldn't concentrate. Closing her eyes, she let the sounds of the morning fill her mind.

Leaning against the balcony railing, her thoughts wandered of their own volition. It seemed that every time she and Roarke got close, something happened to shatter the illusion. Why did he have to leave with Suzanne last night? she agonized. Since he now knew the general was in town, why had it been so imperative that he see him right then? He could have made an appointment for today. Do people really talk business late in the evening? she wondered.

Glittering green eyes blocked all other images in her mind. Who was Suzanne? If they were such good friends, why had she sensed such instant hostility toward her when Suzanne burst in on them. Placing her face into the palms of her hands, she moaned, "How much more can I stand?"

A knock on the door made her heart flutter with panic. If it were Roarke, what would she say to him? The insistent knocking was much louder now and, sighing deeply, she went back into her room to answer the door. She flung it open, and Roarke was leaning against the door frame.

Puzzled by his appearance, Sara stared at him curiously. Never had she seen him so disheveled. His rumpled, dark red silk dressing gown, his uncombed hair, and unshaven face all gave mute evidence that he hadn't had much more sleep than she.

"May I come in for a minute, or are you going to make me stand here in the hall," he asked, his voice devoid of any inflection.

Sara shrugged her shoulders and stepped aside. He slipped passed her and began pacing around the room, unconsciously picking up things and setting them back down without looking at them.

Avoiding his eyes, she closed the door and sat down at the table in front of the window.

"Sara, we need to talk." He walked to the table and leaned over, resting his palms on the top. He sounded tired and, as he stood up to light a cigarette, Sara noticed from the corner of her eyes that his hands shook a little.

He stared out the balcony window, puffing on his cigarette and running his free hand through his hair.

Sara tried not to look at him, but the aura of desolation surrounding him drew her eyes like a magnet. Here was a man who was usually so self-assured and in command of most situations. To see him so rumpled and harried upset her.

"Sara . . ."

She met his eyes. A shock went through her body. She loved him so much, and seeing his obvious distress made her want to reach out and cradle him in her arms. She wanted to croon to him and tell him everything was all right, that she loved him despite all their problems. But she couldn't. Last night stood like a specter between them.

"Last night we tried to bridge the gap between us. I think we made a good beginning." He pulled out a chair and slouched into it. "Look, I told you we'd have to take it day by day." He leaned forward and put out his cigarette. Reaching over, he took her hand tenderly in his. His eyes pleaded with her. "Can we deal with last night?"

Sara looked down at their hands then up at Roarke. "I think we should try. I want to. I didn't get much sleep last night thinking about us."

His grip tightened. "Neither did I, Sara. I am sorry I left you like that last night, but I wasn't thinking straight. I was so surprised that Suzanne had arranged for me to meet with General Robinson, I acted on impulse. I've been in touch with his aide and know for a fact that the general is going to be in town for only two days and he's tied up with meetings at the Pentagon both days. I knew this would be my only chance to see him for quite some time. I wanted to tell you this, but you wouldn't talk to me . . . you locked me out."

"Maybe . . ." she paused. "Maybe I should have let you explain it to me last night," she said in a small voice. "But what about Suzanne?"

Dropping her hand, he demanded, "What about Suzanne?"

"Well," she hesitated, then, determined not to let him hide behind his wall, she stubbornly persisted. "Is she really my friend? Why haven't you mentioned her if she's such a good friend of ours?"

"We've known Suzanne and her late husband for years. My company had a contract to construct several buildings for her father and through business we drifted into a friendship. When her husband died, I helped her sort out his tangled financial affairs. You haven't told me yet, Sara. Can you forgive me for a stupid, impulsive act? I'll try not to let it happen again. I know you were hurt. I saw it in your eyes last night."

100

"Yes, I was, there's no sense in denying it. But if we've come to a better understanding of each other, I guess it's been worth it. Why didn't you tell me about Suzanne? She practically accused you of keeping her away . . . and anyone else who might want to see me."

He grimaced. "Sara, I told you before. Ted felt it was better if you didn't have a lot of people around to confuse you. I was just trying to follow his advice. Besides, Suzanne's accusations don't worry me at all."

Sara sighed again as Roarke walked back over to the window. "I do need time. You and Ted are probably right, Roarke." She reached out and tucked a flower that had fallen onto the middle of the table back into the vase, thinking of all that Roarke had told her. He had apologized and tried to explain why he had left her so abruptly last night. For him, she reasoned, that was a giant step in their relationship. She stood up and walked over to him. "I might not understand or remember that much about your construction business, but I think I realize how important a government contract is. It's just that Suzanne's appearance surprised me, and your going with her was almost like . . . desertion. But I should have let you explain, I'm sorry. Let's try to forget the whole thing."

He turned from the window and just stared at her for several seconds with a peculiar expression on his face. Suddenly he threw his arms open and Sara went to him. Roarke enfolded her against his body and hugged her tightly against him.

She tipped her head back so she could look up into his face. "Why did you look at me so funny?"

Roarke shook his head, smiling. "I just can't get used to the new you."

"Why? Am I so different?"

"As day is from night," he stated, kissing her forehead.

"How am I different?" Sara asked, still puzzled.

"I think I'll let you find that out for yourself. What do you want to do today? How about a picnic? You can bring your sketch pad and we'll find a cozy hideaway where I can lay around and rest while you draw, just like we used to."

"That sounds like fun, but don't you have to be at the office? You've been away for three days!"

"Nope! I called and told them what I wanted done and that I was going to play hooky today." He hugged her. "I want to have fun with my wife!"

Sara kissed Roarke's cheek. "That's a great idea. I'd like to get out; the weather is so beautiful."

"Okay," he said, smiling broadly. "I'll ask Martha to pack a picnic lunch. Can you be ready to leave in about an hour?"

"Sure," she said, smiling back at him.

Roarke kissed her lightly on the mouth and walked toward the door. As he opened it, he paused. "I'll take you to one of your favorite places. Maybe that will help you to remember something. Although I'm still not sure if I want you to remember." He closed the door quietly behind him.

Sara sank back into the chair. *I can't believe I could have been so totally different from the person I am now. What happened and what must I have been like that he's hoping I don't remember anything?* She loved him so much, of that she was positive. She was beginning to think that maybe she didn't want to remember the past either. If the way she is now was so fascinating to him, would he want her if she remembered and changed back?

"No," she said out loud to the room. "I have to remember! I have to be whole! If I can remember and keep Roarke too, it will be an answer to my prayers. But if I remember and can't keep him, I don't know what I'll do, but I won't worry about that now. Regardless of the consequences, I have to know who and what I am."

They walked to the car and Roarke held her hand tightly in his. "Turn around, Sara."

Sara turned slowly in front of him. Her jeans fit snugly across her hips, outlining her slenderness, and her blouse was hot pink with tiny straps that left her shoulders bare to the sun. The blouse hugged her breasts and tapered down until it tucked into her jeans.

"You look terrific, come on!" He laughed as he took her hand again and they got into the car.

They drove on a narrow two-lane highway heavily wooded on either side, and the trees were soft with their newborn leaves. Once in a while she caught a glimpse of houses sitting back away from the road, some with their privacy protected by high walls, and some with giant trees surrounding them. Everything was in bloom, beautiful lush lilacs, gaudy, brilliantly colored azaleas, and fruit trees covered with blossoms from deepest pinks to the whitest whites.

Glancing over at Roarke as he pointed out a particularly colorful display on his side, she smiled to herself. He looks so handsome, she mused. His tight jeans were snug on his thighs and his polo shirt clung to his muscular chest. The wind coming in the open window blew his hair across his forehead. She couldn't see his eyes behind the large dark glasses, but his voice was filled with a boyish excitement.

Chattering with each other about the beautiful scenery and how perfect the weather was for their picnic, they drove for several more miles. Sara was relaxed and happy, treasuring every moment. She didn't know how they got along together before, but she felt like a young girl . . . a young girl in love. Their conversation flowed effortlessly, although they avoided any reference to their past. She was delighted that things were going so smoothly and Roarke was so charming. Roarke turned the car onto a dirt road and drove a little farther. Then he parked the car on the side of the road and turned off the engine.

Sara drank in the beauty that surrounded them. They were on a gently sloping low hill under a small circle of trees and at the foot of the hill was a very old mill, its huge wheel turning slowly in the stream that ran beside it. The murmur of the water splashing on the rocks below added to the sounds of the rustling new leaves on the trees and birds chirping as they busily tended their nests. Some of the trees were dogwood and their branches were dressed in their spring finery. Each branch looked heavy with the blossoms. It was as though they were standing under pink-and-white clouds that had been caught in the trees.

Roarke handed her a blanket to spread out beneath the trees. When she opened the picnic basket, she found that Martha had thought of everything—there was even a bottle of red wine and two glasses. They were ravenous and after they ate, Roarke sat with his back leaning against a tree and Sara sat cross-legged near him and filled their glasses with wine.

She handed Roarke his glass and after taking a few sips picked up her sketch pad. With a few strokes, the hill, the tree, and Roarke leaning against it started coming to life on the paper. Her hand flew, more and more detail becoming apparent. She noticed when she paused that Roarke hadn't taken his eyes off her. Smiling, she asked, "Why such a piercing look, Roarke?"

"I was watching how your beautiful face is so serene in its concentration. You haven't forgotten your art, have you?"

"Apparently not." Her face frowned as she erased a line, then she looked up at him. "Hold still, please, till I get your mouth right." She bowed her head over the drawing. "For some reason, Roarke, my hand and whatever part of my brain that makes it function haven't forgotten. Where are you going? I haven't finished yet!"

He moved over and sat beside her, taking the sketch in his hands. After a few seconds he said, "I'll say you haven't forgotten. In fact, I think you're better than ever. Look at the strength and delicacy you've drawn into that." He pointed to the sketch of the tree.

Smiling gratefully, Sara replied, "I want to start back in oils one of these days. Roarke, there's something I've been wanting to ask you. If we've been separated, why is all my painting equipment at the house?"

Still studying the drawing, he answered casually, "When you

104

left, you only took so much with you. I offered to have your things packed and sent to you, but you kept putting me off, saying you could get new equipment."

Sara watched him with intense interest. Deciding not to pursue the subject further, she reached over and took the sketch pad from him and continued drawing.

They were both silent for several minutes, Sara busily bringing the sketch to life and Roarke not taking his eyes from her face. She felt a little distracted by his staring but became so engrossed by the picture unfolding beneath her pencil that it was as if she were alone.

"Who are you, Sara Alexander?" Roarke asked quietly.

Sara met his eyes and put her drawing down on the ground. "I don't know, Roarke. I really don't know," she repeated softly.

He moved closer to her, reached over, and touched her face. His fingertips traced her jawline and then the edge of her lips. He reached up and gently plucked a flower petal out of her hair that had drifted down from the dogwood. Twirling the petal between his fingers, he studied her face. Sara sat silently, not knowing what to say to him.

"You're the same and yet . . . you're different. I know your face"—he softly touched her cheek—"I know your body . . ." He trailed his finger down her arm and onto her hand then reached out and gently touched her chin. "I know what you look like, I know the taste of your lips. You're the same on the outside, but you're not the same Sara on the inside. Which is the real Sara?"

"I wish I knew, Roarke." She placed her hand over his. "I won't know which one is real until I can remember. I'm a stranger to myself. Some things I know instinctively, like sugar and milk in my coffee, writing with my right hand, my painting. Other things I don't know at all. I . . ."

Roarke gathered her into his arms, gently lay her back on the blanket, and cradled her head in his hand. He looked deeply into her eyes. His dilated pupils appeared to be black instead of the deep blue they usually were. Lowering his lips to meet hers, she responded with such intensity, it sent uncontrollable tremors through her body. She put her arms around him and marveled as his body touched hers. They molded together, neither one wanting to break away or stop the fire that was bursting into flame between them. He ran his hand down her neck and tentatively touched her breasts and when she didn't resist, his hand covered them and tenderly stroked them to response. He moved his lips from hers almost reluctantly then ran kisses down to the hollow of her neck.

Slowly he pulled her shirt out from her jeans and slid his hand underneath it. The touch of his hand against her bare flesh sent fresh shock waves through her body.

Roarke's lips kissed their way from her neck back to her lips and teased them with his tongue. "Sara, I need you." His voice was husky with desire. "I want you with my very being."

"Don't stop touching me, I . . . I want you too, Roarke."

Roarke rolled slightly away from her, leaned on his elbow, and stared at her with an intensity that made her mind reel. His eyes were hooded with passion, his lips soft and full. Fascinated, she watched as he unsnapped her jeans and shivered when his hands glided across the flesh of her hips as he pulled the clothing off. He leaned over and drew the jeans down and over her feet then threw them aside. Running his hands back up her sensitive sides, he lifted her shirt up and over her head.

For what seemed like eternal minutes to Sara, Roarke sat and looked at her nakedness gleaming in the sun. A light breeze blowing through the leaves on the trees threw shadows that mottled her skin. Never taking his eyes from her, he removed his clothing and moved to lie beside her. Slowly he ran his hands from her face down her shoulders, across her breasts, over her stomach, and lightly touched her sensitive thighs.

Sara moaned as he explored places on her body that led to more exploration. Her hands gripped his arms, and then she loosened one hand and felt the strength of his body as she stroked it.

Roarke lowered his head and kissed her, his lips demanding, forceful, and she opened hers to receive the passion that waited for her.

She was oblivious to her surroundings. All she knew or cared about was this love that was lying beside her and then the love she felt inside her.

Their pace was leisurely, not the frantic coupling of their first night. They rose and fell together as they both moved closer to the peak of ecstasy. Roarke's hands didn't cease their searching or caressing, and Sara gripped and kneaded his solid muscles in the throes of her passion.

Groaning, Sara was suddenly flung out to the stars. She soared and imagined she could envision the scene below of their bodies entwined in love's dance.

Roarke lay beside her, the corner of their blanket barely covering his thighs. He seemed to be asleep as she ran her fingertips over the rippling muscles of his stomach. Finally he twitched and let out a chuckle. "Damn it, Sara, you're deliberately tickling me."

"That's right," she replied sweetly. "Don't you think we should get dressed, or do you plan to play king of the jungle all day?"

He sat up, leaned on one elbow, and reached out with his other arm to pull her face to his. Kissing her lingeringly, he ran his tongue across the sensitive inner skin of her lips.

"Oh, no, you don't," she laughed as she drew away. "You're not going to seduce me again, you reprobate. I'm wondering how many people have watched this X-rated show already. Besides, I'm getting sunburned . . . all over!" Laughing again, she grabbed her clothes, ran behind a tree, put them back on, and came back to Roarke, buckling her belt around her waist.

Roarke looked up as he tucked his shirt in his jeans and pulled her into his arms again. "Don't struggle, we're properly clothed.

107

No one saw us. Besides, if they did, how could they deny that it was the most perfect and beautiful thing they had ever witnessed?"

Sara flung her arms around his neck. "Oh, Roarke, what a lovely thing to say. It *was* perfect and beautiful. You make me feel so special."

"Mmmm," he murmured into her hair. "I can't keep my hands off you. You're still the most provocative woman in the world to me." He ran his hands down to cover her breasts, stroking them until they became full with desire. "You are so beautiful, I can't resist you."

Sara smiled and nibbled on his ear lobe. "It must be getting late, don't you think we ought to be leaving? Won't Martha be waiting dinner for us?" Her voice was husky as she whispered into his ear.

He drew back, a seductive smile on his lips. "Dinner! How can you think of dinner? You're going to be my dinner! We're going to go home and I'm going to make love to you all night, just like we used to." His hand was tangled in her hair and he bent to kiss her again.

"Roarke, don't be silly. What would Martha and Bradley think?"

"What do you mean, what would they think? We're married, for Pete's sake. When we get home, we're going to move all your things into my bedroom and from now on you're going to sleep with me!" He nipped the end of her nose with his lips.

"Are you sure about this?" Sara drew her head back and gazed into his eyes. "If I move back into your room that means that our marriage is a reality and all the vows that go with that reality are valid again."

"I wouldn't ask you back into my room unless I was sure," Roarke replied, his voice losing the sexily teasing sound it had had and becoming more serious in tone.

"You may think you're sure, but what if I remember every-

108

thing and revert back to the Sara you closed out of your life two years ago?"

"How many times do I have to tell you we'll face that if it happens!" he replied with a sharp edge to his voice.

"Look, Roarke, we can't do that. There's no 'if' about it. We have to face this now, every day. Making love doesn't erase all the hard facts we're facing. It doesn't erase anything! As a matter of fact, it shouldn't change anything. You said our lovemaking was always great, that it was a good thing even when our marriage was going bad. We just can't run away and make love instead of decisions."

"You're talking nonsense again." Roarke walked to the tree and took a cigarette out of his pocket.

"No, Roarke, I'm not. Are you prepared right now to tell me that when I do remember, and if I'm the old Sara, that you'll still want me to share your bed . . . your life? I need reassurance, Roarke, reassurance from you."

He threw his cigarette down and ground it out with his shoe, twisting the grass beneath his toe. "Maybe you haven't changed as much as I thought, Sara. You have to take apart and psychoanalyze everything we say until I don't know what we're talking about. I'm tired of this. Let's go. You can stay in your own room, but don't expect me to ask again." Roarke picked up their picnic things and began putting them back into the basket.

Sara was aghast. She reached out her hand to grasp his arm, but he shrugged it aside and walked by her to put the things into the trunk of the car. "Roarke, please listen. I'm not . . ."

"I said, we'd better start home." His stern voice was gruff.

Sara knew there was nothing she could say or do that would make the situation any better, so she kept silent and helped him clean up the remaining debris from the picnic, knowing the memory of their love scene would always remain.

Riding back to the house, they were silent, Roarke's hands tightly gripping the wheel, his knuckles white. Sara was miserable and fretful. She shook her head in bewilderment. They were certainly a different couple from the one who had traveled this same road several hours before.

Roarke paused at his study doorway, "If you change your mind, let me know, and we'll talk about it."

Uncontrollable anger seethed through Sara. How dare he be so magnanimous? We'll talk about it! Who does he think he is? Then a calming sheath settled over her. Turning to Roarke, she smiled. "Yes, we'll also discuss your impulse to go out with other women and leave your wife behind."

His lips twisted in a bitter smile as she turned her back on him and started up the stairs, his voice trailing behind her. "Damn you, Sara. I was right! You haven't changed. You are still accusing me of things that are in your imagination."

Sara walked into her room and threw the sketch on the bed. She looked at the drawing of Roarke, propped against the tree, a smile creasing his face. Her mind pictured his tense face and frown as he went into the study. *What a change in just a few hours,* she thought. *It's like he's two people also.* Sitting down in front of her vanity mirror, she examined her reflection intently. Suddenly, as if through a clearing mist, she saw Roarke and herself reflected in the mirror. He was dressed in a tuxedo and she was in a filmy blue gown. She was standing before Roarke with her hands on her hips. "Who was that woman, Roarke?" the reflection was saying and the memory of her voice sounded shrewish.

"Sara, I've already told you who she was," Roarke said impatiently.

"You told me she was 'someone's wife.' She certainly didn't act like 'someone's wife.' " Sara turned on her heel and started pacing the room.

"What exactly do you mean?" Roarke reached out and gripped her arm as she passed him.

"Just what I said. She practically hung on to you the entire evening. It was embarrassing. She acted as though you were her lover or husband and didn't belong to someone else. As a matter

110

of fact, she didn't even acknowledge my presence." Sara's eyes bored into Roarke's.

"Sara, I can't help what that woman does. I did nothing to encourage her. It's nothing that I said or did. I've met the woman twice before and both times her husband was there. You're reading things that aren't there. Furthermore, I don't belong to you. I am not your possession." Roarke removed his tie and shook his head in disgust then turned to leave the room.

"Roarke, don't you dare walk out on me. Every time I turned around, she was beside you. It was as though she couldn't let you out of her sight. You must have done something to encourage her." Sara stamped her foot in impotent fury. "And don't tell me you don't belong to me. You certainly do!"

Roarke pivoted back, anger raging over his face. "Sara, I'm sick of having this conversation every time we go out. I did nothing, I tell you, nothing, to encourage that woman." His voice raised in pitch from exasperation. "I don't care to discuss this anymore."

She went to him and grabbed his arm as he was walking out of the room. "Roarke, I don't believe you. Why would a woman you've only met two times behave around you as she did? I feel sure everyone at that party thought the same thing I did."

"And what was that, Sara?" Roarke asked in a bored tone.

Sara gripped his arm tightly. "Why, that you were lovers, of course."

Roarke shook himself loose of Sara's hand. "I'm tired of your accusations. Every time we go somewhere I have to come home and listen to you accuse me of being someone's lover. I'm tired of this, Sara. It has to stop," he insisted. "I'm tired of your jealousy, I'm tired of your reading infidelity into my every move. I'm tired of this conversation," he said, punching his fist into the door frame in disgust.

"If you're so tired of everything, and that seems to include me, then why don't you leave. Why don't you just leave!" Sara shouted, her face distorted with jealousy and anger.

Roarke stepped back into the room, slamming the door behind him. He reached out and grabbed Sara by the shoulders, jerking her toward him. "Don't push me, Sara. One of these days you'll say it once too often and I *will* leave." He let her go so abruptly she stumbled backward.

Sara recoiled at the fury she knew he was barely controlling. But for some reason she couldn't stop the words that poured out of her mouth. "Don't threaten me, Roarke. I'm not afraid of your threats anymore." She stood rigidly, her eyes flashing, and stared at him haughtily, a grim smile on her face.

He drew his clenched fist back but dropped it, his shoulders slumped, a look of defeat crossed his face. "All right, Sara, you win. I'm leaving. I can't live like this any longer." He slammed the door behind him.

Sara stood in the middle of the room, looking with shock at the closed door. "Roarke, you'll regret this," she screamed. She placed her hands over her face and bowed her head, desolate.

The mist in the mirror cleared and Sara was once more staring at her reflection. Her hand shook as she reached out to touch the mirror where the nightmare scene had been enacted. *Was that me? Was that what our marriage had been?* Sara put her arms down on the vanity top, cradled her head in them, and sobbed as though she would never stop.

CHAPTER EIGHT

Lying with her eyes opened wide, the undulating darkness of her room making her nerves taut, Sara twisted and turned, trying to fall asleep. She yearned for a few hours of blankness, forgetfulness. The sheets clung to her, making her feel sweaty and uncomfortable. Exasperated, she kicked the top sheet to the foot of the bed. What was she going to do? Roarke went out shortly after their return from the picnic, and Sara ate alone in her room. Long after she gave in to her exhaustion and went to bed, she heard him come home. She listened to his footsteps on the stairs and stiffened when they paused by her door. She held her breath, waiting for the sound of the doorknob to turn or of the hinges to rub harshly if the door was opened. But after a few torturous minutes she heard the faint latch of his door and heaved a shuddering sigh.

Staring at the faint light filtering in around the edges of her closed door, she tried to cry, wanted to cry, anything to relieve the pain in her chest and the lump in her throat, but no tears would fall. Her eyes burned from the need to cry. But her pain was too deep and the constant assault on her emotions these past months had just about broken her spirit. She was nearly resigned to whatever contorted design her life would take and felt powerless to stop it.

Sara rolled onto her side and curled into a ball, tucking her feet under her nightgown. This afternoon she had been so happy, but it had been just a mirage created by Roarke's need of her and her love for him. She had been deceived, enticed by a vision of how their life could be. All she had wanted from Roarke was a little reassurance, that if she did have a total reversal of personality when her memory came back he would help her, stand by her, comfort her. His blind spot, his refusal to face the fact that one day her memory would come back, puzzled her. She loved him so much, but the obstacles in their path seemed insurmountable.

Then the specters she had seen in the mirror floated in her mind. The memory of her shrewish, accusing voice echoed in her ears, the kaleidoscope of images filling her brain until she couldn't stand it another second. Putting her hands over her ears and clamping her eyelids shut, she rolled around trying to escape the ghost of the woman she had been.

Could she really blame Roarke for how he behaved? She had been equally guilty of unthinking actions. Even now, with her love for him burning inside her, in a petty act of anger and hurt, she had tried to get even. Her snide remark alluding to his impulsive behavior concerning other women must have seemed to him that she was reverting back to the person she had been. Maybe she was! At last, tears scalded her lashes.

Was there no way out of this mess? "What's going to happen to us?" she whispered to the darkness.

Sara clutched her cup of coffee in both hands, letting its warmth relieve the iciness of her fingers. She was light-headed from lack of sleep and the turmoil that churned inside her.

"Sara!"

Tensing at the sound of his voice behind her, she slowly turned and glanced in his direction. Roarke stood just inside her room, waiting for her response.

She couldn't answer him. Her mouth opened, but no sound came out. He came over and sat across from her. "I knocked, but I guess you didn't hear me."

Sara shook her head and continued to turn her coffee cup in her hands, absorbing the warmth that emanated from the cup.

Roarke scrutinized her face. "You look like hell. Didn't you get any sleep last night?"

"Thanks for the compliment. As a matter of fact, I didn't sleep very well." She rose from her chair and went out onto the balcony. She really wanted to get as far away from Roarke as possible. She wanted to end the misery for both of them.

She felt the warm touch of the sun on her skin, but the heat couldn't penetrate the bleak frigidness beneath. Her misery was bone-chilling. She tilted her face to the sun and closed her eyes.

"Do you want more coffee? There's a fresh pot here."

Sara walked back into her room and sat down at the table again. Roarke poured her coffee, the spout of the pot clinking against the edge of her cup. The silence thickened and was deafening. She glanced at Roarke's face. It was drawn and tense, with dark puffy circles under his eyes. The lines running from his nose to his mouth were deeply creased. He looked haggard, but she couldn't feel even a twinge of concern or sympathy. She was incapable of expending any emotions on him. She didn't have any.

In a raw voice he said, "Martha mentioned you have a doctor's appointment this morning." Roarke leaned back in his chair, his steel blue gaze wary.

Sara nodded. "It's supposed to be my last one."

"I'll drive you in, if it's all right with you. Bradley's busy and I'm free this morning."

"It's all right. I don't care as long as I get there."

"Sara . . ."

"My appointment is at ten, I'd better start getting dressed."

The hum of the motor roared in Sara's ears. The windows were down and a brisk wind blew through the car as they drove onto the George Washington Parkway.

"Would you like to go somewhere for lunch after your appointment?"

Roarke's sudden question surprised her. Figuring that at best,

115

until she got her memory back, their lives would be an armed truce, she was stunned that he'd ask her to go anywhere with him. "Why, Roarke?" she asked with a dead calm.

"I have to take you back home anyway and I thought you might enjoy it. If you don't want to . . . it's up to you."

"I'm just surprised you asked me."

He gave her a quick look. "I don't understand! Why is it so surprising? We used to go out for lunch frequently."

"You also told me once you were sick and tired of my behavior when we went out."

"What do you mean?"

"Oh, Roarke, don't try to hide the past from me!" She pounded her fist on the dashboard. Her voice suddenly went flat. "After we came home yesterday, I was sitting in front of my mirror and like an old movie, I could see the two of us reflected in it. Apparently we'd just come home from a party and were fighting over some woman. It was horrible. I accused you of being her lover and finally I screamed at you and told you to leave and . . . and . . . you did. . . ." Sara's voice trailed away.

"I only left you for a couple of days. I came home to get some clothes and you . . . we made up." His voice was low and Sara looked over at him. She wondered what he had left unsaid.

"Did we fight like that often?" she asked. The vestige of the memory still haunted her. She shuddered when she thought of the anger and viciousness she had witnessed in the mirror.

"Yes," he said so low Sara could barely hear him.

"I see." She turned away from him, devastated by a past she so desperately wanted to remember. "Roarke, how did we stand it? How did we survive, tearing each other to pieces like that?" Sara choked.

"We didn't . . ."

"Are we back to that again, Roarke?"

"Back to what, Sara?" Roarke pulled the car into a parking space in front of Ted's office. Sara mechanically opened the door and, like a robot, got out, and closed it. Leaning in the window, she drew a deep breath. "I guess that's up to you, Roarke." She turned and walked away without waiting for his response.

When she got to Ted's waiting room, she saw there were other people waiting to see him. Spying a vacant chair in the corner, she moved toward it. As she walked passed Ted's receptionist, she murmured her name and asked the woman to let Dr. Maxwell know that she was here for her appointment. She sat for a few minutes, staring at a painting on the wall across the room from her. She had to try to concentrate on something to get her mind quieted down. Ted was so perceptive, she didn't want him to know she was upset.

To distract herself, she picked up a local magazine that was on the table beside her chair. Flipping through the pages, a warning bell went off in her head, and she sat perfectly still, holding her breath, staring at a photograph. The banner headline above the photo was "Who's Kissing Him Now?" It was a local gossip column that had covered a charity event and the picture was of Roarke and Suzanne. She was hanging onto his arm, smiling and gazing up into his eyes.

Sara stared at Roarke's image. He was laughing down at Suzanne, and the photograph caught an aura of intimacy between them. Sara began to read the story that accompanied the picture. The words seemed to leap out at her, scalding her eyes.

Roarke Alexander, the brilliant business executive who parlayed his late father's sagging construction company into a multi-million-dollar empire, can't seem to apply the same expertise to his women. Suzanne Morrison seems to be the one who's kissing him now but, then again, maybe it's his wife, Sara! She was recently in a bad car accident and our sources at the hospital tell us Roarke has been at Sara's side as much as possible. In fact, while she teetered between life and death in Intensive Care, Roarke Alexander never left the hospital . . . he even slept there!

* * *

Sara scanned the story. It told of her leaving Roarke and moving into an apartment they owned in the city. The columnist told of seeing Sara on the arm of many different men but that Roarke's steady date seemed to be Suzanne.

According to gossip, it doesn't seem that a divorce is in the immediate future, but things don't bode well for what has been one of Washington, D.C., society's most popular couples.

Sara dropped the magazine into her lap and leaned her head back against the wall. *Suzanne! Roarke has been dating Suzanne! They both lied to me. Was Roarke so anxious to see Suzanne that he'd have her come to the house pretending to be my friend? And she did it . . . came to see me, saying she was so worried about me. How could she? Unless she was in love with Roarke!*

She looked at the date under the picture. It seared into her brain. He had gone out with Suzanne while she was in the hospital. *That's how much he cared about me! All his reassurance that we'd get through this and he'd help me . . . it was all lies. And Ted said Roarke loved me. What a farce!* Against her will, her eyes moved back to the printed page.

It seems that Marriage-Go-Round Roulette is the new game being played by Washington's super-rich stratum. The game is—who will Roarke choose? Will it be his ailing wife, Sara? Or will it be the glamorous Suzanne, who has been his constant companion for over a year? In this columnist's opinion, Suzanne seems to be the sure winner. Bets, anyone?

Sara felt the blood leave her face. She was stunned and humiliated. How could anyone write such trash? Her whole life, a life she couldn't even remember, was printed in a magazine for everyone to see, for everyone to inspect, dissect. "Oh, what can I do?" Sara whispered aloud.

"Sara . . . Sara, what's wrong?" Ted was kneeling in front of her, rubbing her hands and looking worriedly into her face.

She opened her eyes and looked down at Ted with tears of anguish shimmering in them, ready to spill over. "Oh, Ted." Sara started to sob. The hurt spread its paralyzing fingers around her heart. She wanted to curl into a little ball. Ted gently helped her to her feet and walked her into his office. He guided her to a chair and perched himself on the edge of his desk facing her. Handing her some tissues, he waited for her to pull herself together.

Sara sniffled and looked up at Ted with a watery smile. "I'm sorry, Ted. I'm not sick, åt least not physically. It's this damned article." She waved the magazine under his nose that she held tightly clutched in her hand.

He took the magazine from her and quickly scanned the story then looked over at Sara, sharing a little of her misery. "Damn, I'm sorry, Sara. I didn't know. If I had, I would have thrown the stupid thing in the trash, where, I might add, it belongs." He leaned over and brushed some stray hair off Sara's face. She started crying again. She couldn't cope with his sympathy.

"Everything's there for everyone to see and gossip about. Did you read, people are making bets over who gets Roarke, Suzanne or me? I didn't know," she sobbed. "How could I have known he's been dating her for over a year. Suzanne came to the house the other night, telling me she was my friend . . . my friend?" Sara jumped to her feet and started pacing the office. "He lied to me too. He let her pretend to be my friend. Why? And . . . and, I thought maybe we could mend our marriage, and here my husband has a girl friend."

She swung around and pointed an accusing finger at Ted. "And you knew we were separated before the accident! You knew and didn't tell me, and you call yourself my friend."

"Sara." Ted's face blanched white, sorrow turning his eyes

dark. "Yes, I did know," he said compassionately. "Roarke begged me not to tell you."

"Begged?" Sara broke in. "Roarke begged? The only reason he begged was so he could have his cake and eat it too. And you . . . you're an accessory. How could you do this to me, Ted? How could you?"

The gray head lowered. "I didn't go along with Roarke to hurt you, Sara. How would you have felt if I had told you that you were going home with a husband you've been separated from for some time? Would you have gone? Besides, I'm thoroughly convinced you have to remember on your own. It's the only way it's going to work. I'm sorry, Sara. I would never do anything to hurt you."

She stood by the desk, wringing her hands, ignoring Ted's plaintive explanation. "Did you read what they said about me? It sounds as if I went out with a different man every night. Is Roarke right about me, am I a spider spinning webs, trying to capture any and every man I can? And I thought the love I feel for him would magically make it work out. How naive!" Her voice rose hysterically.

"Sara, Sara, calm down. You have to calm down. Why are you letting this upset you so much? This is just gossip! There has to be an explanation. He doesn't care about Suzanne. I saw a shell of a man wait three days at the hospital for one word about you. I know he loves you. Can't you believe that?" Ted went over to Sara and put one of his huge arms around her shoulders.

She buried her face in his chest for a moment, then lifted her eyes and cried out, "He keeps putting walls between us, Ted. Just when I think I'm getting close he builds another wall. I don't understand him. When I compare the face I see to the one in this picture, it's like he's two different men. What happened to make him like this? Why can't he be honest with me about the past? He's afraid I will remember. Why?" Sara pulled away, holding Ted's eyes with her sad ones. "I'll be honest, Ted. I don't know

120

if I want to remember either. There's something bad in the past that's disturbing to Roarke, and I'm afraid too."

Ted sat down on the edge of his desk again. "Have you remembered anything at all?"

Sara's face contorted with agony. Her mind flashed back to the mirrored images of Roarke and herself. "Oh, yes, and one memory was horrible! I accused Roarke of cheating on me and I didn't stop until I had driven him away. When I asked Roarke what had happened, he said that he left for just a couple of days and when he returned to the house, we made up. But I didn't even know myself, I was this accusing, screaming shrew, driving Roarke out of our home. Did I drive him into Suzanne's arms? Why did I leave him? Was it over her? Or . . . or did I have someone?" Sara wiped her tear-filled eyes. "I'm so afraid. I don't know who I am. Am I the screaming shrew of my memory, or is this who I am? Am I a man-chaser or am I what I feel now? All I want is a life with Roarke and it seems it's too late for that. I don't know who is the illusion and who is real. And now this humiliation." Sara put her head into her hands and cried silently, her shoulders shaking with her sobs. "I can't stand anymore."

Ted took her into his arms and stroked her back, murmuring soothing words.

"If you're finished examining Sara, I'd like to take her home." Roarke stood woodenly in the doorway of Ted's office, his face etched with fury.

Sara's mouth opened in shock and Ted dropped his arm from around her and walked over to Roarke with his hand outstretched. "Good morning, Roarke."

Roarke's eyes were smoldering. For one breathless second Sara thought Roarke would ignore Ted's extended hand, but after a slight hesitation they shook hands perfunctorily. "Good morning," Roarke said shortly. He looked at Sara, who was standing motionless in the middle of the office. "Are you ready to leave, Sara?"

She glanced from Roarke to Ted with panic. "Yes, Roarke,"

121

Ted interjected. "She's ready to leave. She's doing just fine. If she would just gain a little more weight, I'd be very pleased with her." Sara sagged with relief. Ted didn't mention that he hadn't examined her.

"Fine. I'll wait for you in the car, Sara," Roarke said curtly. He nodded to Ted and left them both standing in the middle of the office, staring after him.

"I think Roarke misunderstood what he saw when he walked in. He misread my sympathy for you and made something more of it. I'm so sorry, Sara." Ted shook his head in bewilderment.

"Yes, I know. He doesn't trust me and I doubt if he'll listen to me." Sara gathered up her purse. "May I keep this?" she asked, holding up the crumpled magazine. At Ted's nod Sara stuffed it into her purse.

"Sara, one of these days when you're in town, stop by and I'll do your checkup. You don't have to make an appointment." Ted kissed her on the forehead. "Have faith, Joe," he said, smiling at her tenderly. Sara smiled weakly and with the tips of her fingers she touched his cheek affectionately.

Slowly walking toward Roarke's car, she tried to calm herself and delay the confrontation she felt would occur. She didn't know what kind of scene she'd have to face with him. The sad thing was she didn't care anymore. She was tired of explaining, proving, watching every move she made and every word she spoke.

Her heart had been like a fallow field waiting to be planted, planted with the seeds of her past life. The seeds of love that were already there, waiting to be nurtured, wanting to grow and blossom, were shriveling from neglect.

She climbed into the car and sat rigidly beside him, not uttering a sound. She didn't look at him but kept her eyes straight ahead and stared blindly out the windshield. She was determined not to be defensive.

Roarke didn't talk either. He eased the car into the traffic and concentrated on his driving until they were out of the city.

Sara's heart sank to the pit of her stomach when she saw Roarke pull the car off the highway and park beside the road. He shut off the engine, turned in his seat, and stared at her unblinkingly. "I thought you had an appointment for a check-up?" His voice was cold and felt like a dagger of ice penetrating her.

Sara, equally cool and controlled, met his eyes, at least she hoped she appeared that way. "I did have an appointment," she stated shortly.

Roarke reached across and gripped her arm. "Then why was he making love to you?" he demanded, his tone menacing.

Sara jerked her arm away. "He was not making love to me. I was upset and crying. Ted was just trying to be sympathetic." She sat rigidly in the seat and faced him without flinching from his hostile, angry eyes. She was angry now! How dare he accuse her of being unfaithful, he of all people! And, of all things, in a doctor's office with a waiting room full of people. Maybe she wasn't a shrew after all. Maybe he had always accused her of being unfaithful. Maybe she had been retaliating on his level.

"Why were you crying?" His voice lost its edge of harshness.

Sara reached into her purse and threw the magazine at him. "Because of this!" She turned her back on him.

After several tense minutes Roarke's voice filtered through her angry thoughts. "Where in the hell did you find this?" He sounded drained and leaden.

"I was looking through it while I was in Ted's waiting room. I won't lie to you; it upset me. I started crying and Ted took me into his office. I guess he didn't want me to make a scene in front of his other patients." Sara continued to face the window.

"It's just a trashy gossip column. Why would this upset you to the point that Maxwell would have to put his arms around you to make you feel better?"

"Well, in the first place, I didn't know you and Suzanne were dating. And in the second place, people are taking bets whether Suzanne or I will win the first prize! Our lives have been exposed

123

to anyone who can pay the money to buy this garbage. And what about where it says that Suzanne is your constant companion, even while I was in the hospital listening to all those pep talks from you. Is it true? Whose friend is she, Roarke? Did you date her while we were married? 'Marriage-Go-Round Roulette!' It's more like musical beds!"

"Musical beds? That's more in your line, Sara, not mine." He threw the magazine back at her and restarted the engine.

Sara kept her back to him the remainder of the ride home. She couldn't have spoken if she had tried. Anger and hurt stuck in her throat, and she was surprised she could even breathe.

He drove up in front of the house and stopped the car but didn't turn off the engine. "I'm not coming in. I'm going back to the office. I don't know when I'll be home." His voice was cold and he kept his eyes straight ahead, not looking at Sara.

Sara grabbed the magazine and stuffed it back into her purse, got out of the car, and slammed the door. She practically ran into the house past a surprised Bradley, who had opened the door for her, and went straight to her room, closing the door and locking it behind her.

Leaning against the locked door, staring into space, Sara was too numb to feel anything. If only her memory would come back, she could leave Roarke, leave all this distress, jealousy, and anger.

She threw her purse on the bed and flung herself down in the chaise. She sat staring glassy-eyed in front of the blank TV. Suddenly the TV was filled with shadowy apparitions of Roarke and Suzanne. They were dressed in evening clothes and groups of other people were milling around them. Then a couple walked out of the crowd toward them. It was she with a very attractive man. The man's arm was draped over her shoulder and he was laughing down at her, his eyes filled with warm affection.

Sara was mesmerized and became the audience to the scene being played out before her on the TV.

The Sara on the screen glanced up and saw Roarke and Suzanne standing in front of her. "Hello, Sara. I didn't know you had been invited to the party," Suzanne purred, holding onto Roarke's arm possessively.

"Hello, Roarke, Suzanne. I'm always invited to the Hedges' parties. Linda and I went to school together. How's Martha, Roarke?" Sara turned her attention to Roarke and met his hostile eyes. She deliberately cut Suzanne out of the conversation.

Roarke looked from Sara to the man who had pulled her closer to him. "I see you have another friend," Roarke said, barely concealing the disgust in his voice.

"Oh, I'm sorry, Brian, this is Roarke." Sara smiled up at Brian with affection that the watching Sara felt sure was for the benefit of their audience. The TV Sara still ignored Suzanne.

Roarke sloughed off the introduction and answered Sara's earlier question. "Martha and Bradley are fine. I'll tell the   you asked about them. Now if you'll excuse us?" Roarke put h   hand over Suzanne's that held him tightly at the crook of his arm.

"Good night, Roarke," Sara answered.

Roarke and Suzanne started moving through the crowd of people, but before Sara could turn around, Suzanne was back without Roarke.

"Sara, I think you should seriously consider having Martha come to work for you when Roarke and I are married. I will not tolerate that woman in my house," Suzanne confided.

Pulling herself up to her full height, which was still inches shorter than Suzanne, Sara smiled one of her sweetest smiles. "Suzanne, you're forgetting one little thing. Before you can marry Roarke, he should be divorced from me." Sara moved to stand closer to Suzanne, placed her hand on Suzanne's arm, and bent her head toward the woman, as if to share a secret. "One thing you can count on"—Sara patted Suzanne's arm—"Martha will never be out of a job with Roarke." Sara laughed merrily as a flush burned its way up Suzanne's neck. "We live in hope, don't we?" Still laughing, she grabbed Brian's arm, turned on her heel, and left Suzanne glaring after them, seething with anger.

Sara's vision cleared and she was again staring at the blank TV. *Was I really that spiteful? Was . . . no . . . is Roarke in love with Suzanne? Has he asked Suzanne to marry him when I divorce him?*

She flung herself out of the chaise and started pacing the room. *I can't stay cooped up in here.* Sara looked out the window. *I have to get out of here!* She didn't see anyone on her way out of the house and closed the front door quietly behind her.

Walking into a wooded area, she stopped to watch some squirrels playing tag among the trees. She sat down on the fresh green grass quietly, not wanting to frighten the little animals away. Their antics became more outrageous when they realized they had an appreciative audience. The sun was hot and its light shining through the leaves dappled the ground with shadows that shimmered and bounced around where she sat. The squirrels became more curious and moved closer to her. She held out her empty hands to show them she didn't have any food, but it didn't seem to matter to them. They cavorted and played for her benefit anyway.

Suddenly there was something behind her. She sat rigidly as her heart pounded with fear when she felt a cold, wet something touch her shoulder. Turning her head very slowly, she looked up into the brown eyes of a huge black dog. Sara didn't know what to do. If she got up and tried to run, the dog might attack her. She didn't move a muscle. After sniffing at her hair for several seconds, the dog walked around and sat down in front of her. Extending his paw to Sara, he waited for her to respond to his gesture of friendship.

Sara giggled with relief and at the comical horse of a dog wanting to be friends. She solemnly took the paw extended to her and shook it. "Hello, I'm pleased to meet you. I'm even more pleased that you decided to be friends. I don't quite know what I would have done if you hadn't."

The dog stood up and put his nose into Sara's face and gave her several sloppy kisses on her cheek. Sara fell back laughing onto the ground and tried to ward off any more affection from her new friend.

She sat up and saw that the dog had picked up a stick in his mouth, his eyes begging Sara to throw it for him. "I don't feel that saying no to you would be a good idea, so I'll play."

Sara threw the stick until she felt she couldn't lift her arm anymore. Sitting down, she told the dog it was time for some rest and was surprised that the dog immediately dropped the stick. He came over beside her and dropped to the ground. He lay down with his head in her lap and Sara patted the silky black neck.

After a few minutes the dog's ears perked up and he jumped to his feet beside Sara with an air of expectation. She glanced over her shoulder and saw Roarke casually leaning against a tree, smoking a cigarette. Realizing Sara had seen him, he walked slowly over to where she sat on the ground.

The dog danced around Sara as though he were trying to tell Roarke about his new friend. Roarke patted the dog. "Good boy, Zoe," he said, then turned his attention from the dog to Sara. "Why didn't you tell someone where you were going?"

"I didn't know I had to report my moves to anyone. From now on I will," Sara retorted.

Roarke sat down on the ground beside Sara, and the dog lay in front of them. "You don't have to report to anyone," Roarke snapped at her. "Martha was panicked when I came in. She said you had been gone all afternoon and no one had seen you leave the house. I'm not talking about reporting in, I'm talking about a little consideration for others."

Sara looked into eyes that were cold and a face that was impassive. "I'll apologize to Martha. I didn't mean to worry her, but I just couldn't stay cooped up in the house any longer. Besides, I made several new friends today, including this black beauty." She pointed to the dog.

"Zoe makes friends quite easily. Since when were you interested in making friends with him? A little over two years ago you

127

told me you didn't even want him in the house." Roarke sounded perplexed and he stroked the dog's black head protectively.

"He's your dog then?" Sara asked. She reached over and also petted the animal. Zoe lay perfectly still with his head between his huge paws. But his eyes moved back and forth from one human to the other. Occasionally, as though beyond his control, his tail would flick back and forth.

"I bought him as a gift for you. I was traveling a lot and I thought a dog would be good protection for you, but the first time he had an accident in the house, you threw him out."

A vague memory flitted into her thoughts then grew stronger until she remembered the dream she had of Roarke giving her a package. "I wasn't dreaming then," she murmured.

"What did you say?" Roarke's gruff voice halted the hope that had been blossoming.

Sara looked back up into his eyes and winced at the frigid gaze that iced her heart. "Do you allow him in the house now?" she asked softly, stroking the silky head once more.

"Yes, but he's kept either in my study or in the kitchen. He's gotten used to having his movements restricted. Are you ready to go home?" He stood up, brushed off his trousers, and waited for her to answer.

Sara stood up and walked beside Roarke in silence. At the house Roarke left Sara standing in the hall and went into his study without a word to her. Zoe followed his master, but Sara saw the dog turn around and look at her with his soft brown eyes and a slight movement of his tail.

Slowly she climbed the stairs, deep in thought, went to her room, and walked out onto the balcony. Sitting back in the chaise longue, she let the tumultuous thoughts flow freely. She could not go on like this. Whether her memory returned or not, she'd have to leave this house. Whether she loved Roarke or not was immaterial now. Her flashbacks of memories, the story in the magazine, and the pendulum of Roarke's moods swinging her from anger to love and back again made her realize they

128

couldn't build any kind of life together. The past would always stand between them.

The thought cut through her like a knife. Roarke's laughing face floated in front of her eyes. She ached with her love for him. *If only I could bring laughter to his face. But instead I fill him with anger and bitterness. I have to find some other place to go. Maybe without my presence here he could start rebuilding his life and I could find mine.* She hit her fist on the arm of the longue. She'd give him a divorce! She wouldn't play games with him anymore as she apparently had done in the past.

Sara stood and leaned against the railing that edged the balcony. *I love him so much,* she cried to herself. *Why does it have to be this way? Why can we find happiness only with other people?* She knew then that they could never be anything more than intimate strangers.

CHAPTER NINE

Pulling back the heavy damask drape, Sara looked out at the vast dark sky sprinkled with stars. The glow from the city lit up the horizon, fringing the distant low hills. She opened the sliding window and stepped out onto the balcony.

Roarke wasn't home. He left when they got back to the house. She wondered if he was going to stay out all night. His absence aroused her curiosity. But his not being here gave her some time to think about what she was going to do and how she was going to accomplish it. The hardest decision had been made earlier; she would divorce him. Now she needed to decide how to eliminate herself from his life.

A mockingbird trilled, echoing through the quiet night. Its mimicry of another's love call struck a poignant chord in Sara. She shivered at the melancholy sound. Nostalgia filled Sara's heart, a nostalgia she didn't understand. She pictured long lazy summer evenings sitting on a veranda, sipping a cooling drink; walking through lush woods filled with wild flowers; feeding a horse sugar lumps taken from her pocket and the horse nuzzling her neck. Sweet fragrant nights, listening to the crickets and cicada chirping their summer serenade in the dusk, fireflies flitting in and out of the lilac bushes, lighting pathways for others.

This nostalgia made Sara ache with wistful longings. She couldn't remember actually doing or seeing these things and wanted desperately to be able to remember. Somewhere she must have experienced all of this, otherwise why would she have such a longing?

All these feelings made her more resolute in her decision to find somewhere else to go. She needed to belong somewhere. She didn't belong here! The pressure in this house was intolerable. It was like living with a time bomb. Roarke's indifference to her pleas for understanding was worse than his accusing her of betraying his trust. It was a wall she couldn't break through.

She didn't know where to go. She couldn't ask Martha too many questions because she didn't want anyone to know she was planning to leave. She'd have to think of a good excuse to leave the house, one that didn't raise any suspicions with anyone.

A restlessness suddenly seized her. She had made a decision and the futility of not being able to carry it through right this minute frustrated her. She went back into her room and saw the crumpled magazine laying on the table. Picking it up, forced to punish herself, Sara reread the article about Roarke and Suzanne. It was self-inflicted torture, but each time she read through it and remembered the scene with Roarke on their way home from Ted's office, her determination to leave became stronger. Suddenly one line from the story swam in front of her eyes. "Sara Alexander had taken up residence in the couple's Washington apartment."

Sara knew where she would go! She'd find out where the apartment was, get the keys, and stay there until she could figure out her next move. There must be some way for her to get the information without anyone questioning her motives.

Sara sat for hours, plotting ideas, then quickly rejecting the plots. The agitation of wanting to do something positive, immediately, and knowing she'd have to wait until tomorrow made her pace the room. She had to forcibly subdue the impulse to run, run away from the house, run away from Roarke, run away from herself.

Spotting headlights coming up the driveway, she hastily moved away from the window. She didn't want Roarke to know she was still awake. The thought of facing his cold insensibility or his self-righteous condemnation left her shaking and sick to her stomach.

Turning out all the lights, she listened for the sounds of Roarke's presence in the house. Sitting on the edge of the bed for what seemed an eternity, she heard nothing. After a while her curiosity overcame her reticence to confront Roarke and she tiptoed out of her room and silently trod down the stairs.

There was no one in the hall, but a lighted sconce cast her dancing shadow on the walls, giving her an eerie feeling of not really being alone. Sara proceeded stealthily to Roarke's study and stood at the door listening for any sounds that might emanate from inside the room. She heard nothing.

Very cautiously turning the knob, inching the door open, she prayed Roarke wasn't in the study. If he were in there, she'd have to think of a good reason for her intrusion into his private sanctum. Peering around the edge of the door, she saw that the only light in the room came from a small desk lamp someone had left on. It shed its light grudgingly over the top of the desk, but the glow dissipated as it vied with the darkness in the rest of the room, and in the corners, darkness took over. She looked around, and as far as she could tell the study was empty. Feeling some of the tension leave her tightened muscles, Sara moved into the room then gasped as a shadow moved from behind the desk. She laughed in relief to see Zoe, the huge great Dane, standing before her, his tail wagging in excited recognition. Bending down and stroking him lovingly, she suddenly became aware of just how lonely she was.

"Well, old boy, you've won me over. I abjectly apologize for my past mistakes," Sara whispered to the prancing dog. "Come on, Zoe, tonight you share my room." Sara encouraged the dog with a low whistle and after quietly closing the study door, they went silently up the stairs.

The strain of the day caught up with her, and after a few comforting words to the confused but excited dog, Sara went to bed. Zoe put a cautious paw on the footboard of her bed and she pretended not to notice when the dog climbed up onto the bed and lay down. She chuckled at how the huge animal seemed to control his movements in slow motion as he maneuvered his gigantic body until he was comfortable.

Later, when Roarke couldn't find the dog, he slowly opened Sara's door and heard the rumble of Zoe's protective growl. Roarke entered the room and reassured him that he meant her no harm. As he left the room, Roarke stood in the doorway staring at the woman lying in the bed, her hair spraying over the pillow like golden strands of silk in the light from the hallway. "Please don't remember yet, Sara," he whispered. Shaking his head and shrugging his shoulders, he quietly closed the door behind him.

"Miss Sara, what is that beast doing up here?" Martha's voice filtered through Sara's deep sleep. Blinking her eyes, Sara sat up and laughed at the expression of horror on Martha's face.

"Zoe and I are friends and I invited him up here." Sara looked lovingly at the dog who was standing across the doorway barring Martha's entry into the room.

"Please tell your friend to let me come in," Martha protested. "I want to set this tray down before I drop it on the floor."

"Good boy, Zoe. Now go downstairs and get your breakfast." Sara threw her head back and laughed as the dog pranced from the room but not without a triumphant look at Martha.

"Why anyone would want a beast like that! It's not a dog, it's as big as a pony." Martha set the tray down and poured Sara a cup of coffee. Sara knotted her robe as she sat down at the table.

Sara decided now was as good a time as any to try out the plan she had formulated the evening before. She just hoped she could fool Martha and get the information she needed. Martha must not get too suspicious. This was Sara's only chance, and if Martha would get suspicious, Sara probably would never get away. Martha would tell Roarke and he would probably stop her.

"Martha, do you know where the keys to the apartment in Washington are kept?" she asked with what she hoped was a light curiosity in her voice.

"Why would you want the keys to the apartment?" Martha questioned with one eyebrow raised.

Sara took a deep breath and put her shaking hands in her lap, hoping she could stay calm. "Well, Roarke told me that's where I had been staying while we were separated. I'm curious about the place." Sara propped her chin in her hand, trying to maintain her casual pose.

"So you found out! How?"

"Roarke told me, Martha."

"Oh, Miss Sara." Martha shook her head. "At first I felt guilty about not telling you. But when Mr. Roarke explained to us what the doctor told him, that you should remember by yourself, I went along with it. I hope you're not mad at me."

Sara went over to the older woman and put her arm around her shoulder. "Don't look so sad, Martha. I'm not mad at you. I know you did what you felt was right."

"Right or wrong, only time will tell, Miss Sara."

"Yes, time . . . so much time," Sara murmured. "Well, maybe we can help time along. Do we have keys? It might help me to remember something if I saw the apartment."

"You're right, it might do you good to go there." Martha brightened considerably. "I have extra sets to all the keys downstairs. Mr. Roarke keeps extra keys here and at his office. When would you want to go into town?" Martha asked.

"I was wondering if Bradley would mind running me in today? I'd kind of like to spend the day rummaging through things. I'll phone Roarke at the office and ride back home with him." Sara was relaxing and her hands stopped trembling. She felt triumphant. Despite her twinge of guilt at having to deceive Martha, she succeeded in waylaying her curiosity.

"I'll look through the keys and bring the set up to you," Martha said over her shoulder as she walked out of the room.

"I think I'll come down with you. You never know, maybe going through the keys will jog something in my memory. I'll dress and be right down." Sara didn't wait for Martha to leave the room before she pulled out a pair of jeans and a shirt from the closet, dressed quickly, and ran downstairs.

Standing beside Martha in the kitchen, she watched with building excitement as Martha pulled a huge ring of keys from one of the cabinet drawers. "Let's see, these are extra car keys, this is an extra key to the house . . ." Martha was ticking off each key on the ring. "This is to the town house in Annapolis . . ."

"The town house in Annapolis?" Sara asked incredulously.

"Yes, Mr. Roarke bought it for your second anniversary because you fell in love with Annapolis. You two spent lots of weekends there during the summers." Martha smiled at fond memories of long ago. "Here's the key to the apartment." She held up her discovery.

Sara took the key from Martha's extended hand. She had another idea, but she had to think of a way to get Martha out of the kitchen immediately. "Martha, could you please find Bradley and tell him I'd like to leave as soon as possible."

Martha nodded her head and went out the kitchen door. Sara moved over to the window. She wanted to make sure she had enough time to carry out her idea. She watched Martha walking through the yard toward the garage. Going back to the drawer, she removed the key to the Annapolis home from the ring. Luckily Martha hadn't wasted any time in leaving the kitchen, Sara breathed a sigh of relief. She was so afraid she would forget which key was the right one, only having a moment to observe the position of the key on the ring. She replaced the key ring in the drawer and closed it. Quickly slipping the keys into her pocket, she looked around, then left the kitchen and went up to her room.

Once again in her bedroom, she knew she couldn't take anything with her. Her heart turned over with sadness because her

135

life, the part she could remember, was coming to an end. She stood out in the hall sighing, and closed her bedroom door firmly, hoping she could close out her longing for Roarke just as firmly, just as finally.

Bradley was waiting for her at the front door of the house. "Do you want me to wait for you and bring you back home, Miss Sara?"

"No, Bradley, I'll call Roarke," Sara said with a sigh.

On the ride into town she sat quietly in the corner of the back seat of the huge car. Bradley didn't break through her thoughts with any chatter as he was concentrating on the traffic. The sunlight flickered through the window and across her pensive face. Sara's thoughts were tumultuous and occasionally she would give her head a shake as though to clear her mind.

After he told her the apartment number, Bradley pulled away from the curb. Sara stood in front of the tall double doors of the highrise building. As she looked up at the balconies towering over her, she shuddered with apprehension.

People were brushing by her, singly and in groups, each seeming to know where they were going and where they had been. Sara wanted to call Bradley back; she wanted to retreat to her room at the house. It was her security and now she was on her own, there was no place else she could go. She knew she could call Ted Maxwell but hesitated to involve him. Sara knew if Roarke would try to find her he would go to Ted, feeling that he was the only outsider Sara would go to for help.

Bracing her shoulders, she pulled the huge door open and walked through it with her chin held high. As she walked through the lobby, several people smiled and said hello to her. None of their faces were familiar, but she did manage a weak smile in return. She tried to act nonchalant as she waited for the elevator, gazing up at the floor indicator panel as each number flashed. The elevator doors opened and she silently rode the cab to the floor the apartment was on. Walking down the long corridor, she found the correct door, unlocked it, and timidily slipped in. A sigh escaped her lips; the apartment seemed empty.

Sara went from room to room. There was no one in the apartment and nothing she saw brought back any memories to her. The closet in the bedroom, like the one at Roarke's home, was filled with beautiful clothes. Another door off the hall was closed and locked and Sara fleetingly wondered what secrets were behind it. There were photographs in the different rooms. Surprised, Sara examined them closely. They were all of Roarke.

The furniture looked comfortable and the kitchen had every conceivable modern appliance. It puzzled Sara that the apartment was spotless. It didn't have the air of a place that had been unoccupied for several months. Was Roarke staying here occasionally or had he lent the apartment to someone? On the other hand, she thought, he probably hadn't let anyone else stay here because there were only women's clothing hanging in the closets. It could be that someone came in and cleaned it once in a while.

Sara sat in the living room drinking a cup of tea, trying to soothe her jangled nerves as she watched the sunset behind the Kennedy Center through the huge wall of windows. It was getting late and Roarke would be coming home. When she wasn't with him, they'd worry and start a search. Naturally he would come here first, so she had to think fast. She didn't want a confrontation with him until she had a plan for her future. She had the key to the town house in Annapolis, but she had no idea how to get there or where it was. She couldn't just go around Annapolis trying the key in every door.

Hopelessness was beginning to overwhelm her again. She couldn't escape Roarke if she didn't know where she was going to stay. She had looked at every photo in the apartment and had gone through every paper she could find, but there was nothing to give her a hint of the address of the town house. All her reading and searching hadn't brought any recollection of any of her past. She was caught in a trap. The trap of not being able to remember, the trap of her love for Roarke and Roarke's antagonism toward her.

The sound of the telephone shattered the silence and Sara gave a start. She stared at the phone. She didn't hear the ringing, instead she was listening to the snap of the trap as it clamped shut on her. She couldn't answer it, couldn't go near it. The search for her had begun. It would be only a matter of time before Roarke came to the apartment looking for her.

She got to her feet and started pacing the room, her eyes darting around like a cornered animal seeking escape. The phone rang several times and each time it rang Sara felt surer than ever that Roarke was on his way. Slumping into a chair, she put her head in her hands. Where could she go to escape him? If only he loved her, she wouldn't have to run away from him. But he didn't love her, didn't believe in her, and she couldn't live with her suspicions and his unfair accusations.

Sara gasped as she heard a key being fitted into the lock of the front door. She bolted out of the chair, expecting Roarke to come in and order her back home. Forcing herself to turn and face him, the front door opened slowly, and Suzanne entered the foyer. Sara felt the breath rush from her lungs.

Suzanne stopped abruptly when she saw Sara standing in the middle of the living room. She closed the door and leaned against it, twirling the keys in her fingers. "May I ask what you're doing here?" she asked, looking puzzled.

Attempting to pull herself together, Sara turned and sat back down in the chair. Suzanne's unexpected appearance made Sara very apprehensive. She knew that Suzanne could mean only more problems for her in achieving her freedom. Taking the time to verbally spar with this woman meant precious moments wasted in her flight from Roarke.

"I could ask you the same thing, since this is my home. Why are you here? Roarke's not here, and I know it's not concern for me that brought you here." She crossed her legs, trying to look relaxed.

Suzanne sauntered into the room, threw the keys she had in her hand into a little bowl on a small table, kicked off her shoes, and gracefully sank down on the sofa. "You're mistaken, Sara, this used to be your home. It's mine now," she drawled. "I see you've made yourself quite comfortable," she commented, glancing at Sara's teacup.

"Your home! It's not your home; it's Roarke's and mine. You have no business being here," Sara said indignantly.

Suzanne languidly rose from the sofa. "All right, Sara, since we're both dropping our little poses, let's get down to brass tacks. I knew once Roarke wasn't around you'd drop your lost little girl act. That's why I had to come to the house the other night. I wanted to see how well you played your role. And I must say, Sara, your talents are lost on painting. You should have been on the stage. Poor Roarke, he's such a sucker where you're concerned. He always lets pity overcome his better judgment when you're in the picture. I'm tired of you using Roarke; it's time that it stopped. Roarke and I are going to marry, and there's not a thing you can do about it." Suzanne stood in front of Sara, her hands on her hips, tapping her stockinged foot with impatience.

Sara couldn't meet the other woman's eyes. She was totally confused. What was she talking about? Had Roarke really moved Suzanne into this apartment? On those nights he supposedly worked late, were they spent here with Suzanne?

Suzanne sat down again on the sofa. "When it was made clear to Roarke how badly injured you were and when you were released from the hospital you would need constant care, he made the decision to move you back into the house. I moved out and moved in here. Of course it was only to be a temporary move, but you just couldn't resist using the situation to your advantage. You know how responsible Roarke feels for you since you have no family. I'm sick of you taking advantage of that fact; you're a big girl now. It's time for you to stand on your own two feet. Roarke and I are eager to put the past behind us and start our new life together." Suzanne sat with her hands folded in front of her face, her nose covered by the apex of her fingertips. The only feature of Suzanne's face Sara could see were her glowing catlike eyes that were locked onto Sara's face with an imperious gleam.

"What are you talking about? I don't understand. If you're telling me the truth, why wouldn't Martha tell me you were living here? She gave me the key," Sara gasped.

Suzanne threw her head back in deep soft laughter that purred through the room. "Darling, why would Roarke have to ask permission from a servant to do what he wants, when he wants? You're more naive than I thought." Her laughter ceased suddenly and her eyes pierced Sara's. "Yes, that's it. It's all part of the role you're playing. The helpless child with no memories."

"Suzanne, what do you mean, my role as a helpless child with no memories. I can't remember—"

"This is beginning to bore me, Sara," Suzanne interrupted. "What are you doing here? I know Roarke doesn't know where you are because he would have stopped you from coming here. For some reason he has this big-brother protectiveness where you're concerned." She chuckled. "I can just see the expression on Roarke's face if you had told him you were coming to this apartment. He's so sure that you've really lost your memory that he wanted to keep you from finding out that he's in the process of divorcing you to marry me. Your doctor told him some nonsense that if he told you of our plans, it would be more than you could stand. He feels that the accident has put you in such a state of shock that any more emotional strain might put you over the edge. What nonsense. We both know how strong you are!"

Sara watched Suzanne pull a dark cigarette from her purse. Suzanne was very calm and very sure of herself. Someone in this room was insane, and Sara's insides began to shake. *Is everything Suzanne telling me the truth? Is she living here? Are she and Roarke in love?* It had to be true. *I saw the photo in the magazine with my own eyes. Suzanne thinks that I don't have amnesia and can remember everything. I don't recognize anything here, so how can I be positive she's not living here? It must be true!*

Suzanne's slight smile as she exhaled the smoke stabbed at Sara's heart. "Give up, Sara. Roarke put you out of his life long ago. Why do you insist on torturing the man? You know how responsible he feels for you. Why do you persist in continuing this charade and reinforcing his feeling of obligation? If he felt any love for you, it died long ago. Why can't you step gracefully out of his life? You certainly haven't been an asset to him, I can tell you that! Your antics over the past two years have brought him so much unwanted attention. How do you think he felt with you going out with different men all the time? Poor Roarke, the talk he had to put up with behind his back about his wife having round heels!"

Sara stared at Suzanne in stunned disbelief. "Other men? I couldn't have been like that!"

Suzanne leaped to her feet. "Why are you keeping up this lost-memory ploy?" she cried heatedly. "I told you, you can fool your doctor, you can try to fool Roarke, but you can't fool me. Roarke doesn't love you. How can you want to keep a man tied to you who doesn't want you? He has bitterly regretted his marriage to you and yet you won't let go. You keep him hanging around for your sick pleasure and drag him through all your escapades with you." Suzanne was shouting and Sara winced at the fury in her eyes. "I hate you, Sara. I hate you because of what you've done to Roarke. You've single-handedly almost ruined his business, made him the laughing stock of his friends and business associates, and just when he was going to put you out of his life forever, you have this automobile accident. It wouldn't take much convincing for me to believe you had that 'accident' on purpose." Suzanne was calmer and stood towering over a shocked Sara still riveted in her chair. "It does seem ironic that you'd have an accident the very day you were to be served with Roarke's divorce papers." Suzanne leaned down, placing her hands on the arms of the chair on either side of Sara, trapping her in the seat, forcing her to look up at Suzanne. "Give up, Sara, you've lost!"

Sara stared into Suzanne's feline eyes and what she saw convinced her Suzanne was telling her the truth. She didn't see hate or anger in Suzanne's eyes. Sara saw pity. Suzanne pitied her!

Suzanne released her hold on the chair and walked back over to the sofa and curled her body into the deep cushions.

Sara was paralyzed. After a few moments she stood, her legs trembling and threatening not to hold her up. But she braced herself and with her back straight and her head held high Sara picked up her purse from the table in the foyer, opened the door, and left the apartment. She was determined Suzanne would not see the pain she had inflicted on her or the defeat and humiliation that she knew showed in her eyes.

Outside the closed apartment door Sara leaned weakly against the wall, trying to pull herself together. Her hands were shaking badly and her knees felt like they would not support her. The churning of her stomach was welcome, as it momentarily took her mind off her breaking heart. Shame and humiliation washed over her, and her face flamed with the memory of Suzanne's words.

Sara took a deep breath and walked toward the elevator, her one coherent thought was to escape Suzanne's triumph and to leave before Roarke would come looking for her. She couldn't face him now, she doubted if she could ever face him. Had she really humiliated him? Had she made him the laughing stock of his friends? All those . . . those men in her past! No wonder he doesn't want me to get my memory back! No wonder he wants . . . wants Suzanne!

The elevator door closed, leaving Sara in momentary solitude. She leaned her head against the cool wall of the cab, beating it with a white-knuckled fist. *My God, what kind of a cruel, sadistic person am I?* Hysteria tried to bubble up inside her, but she knew she must keep it in check. She didn't want to look as sick as she felt when she walked through the lobby.

The elevator doors parted and she stepped out of the cab. Moving through the lobby like a robot, she stared straight ahead, concentrating on putting one foot in front of the other and getting out of the building quickly. Outside, the warm evening breeze ruffled her hair and felt cool on her face. She looked around her at the traffic-filled street. *Where can I go?* she thought, with panic rising in her throat.

She walked around the corner of the building and for several moments leaned against the side of it. There has to be one answer to this. *I am crazy. No, I can't think about that right now. I have to focus on what I'm going to do. I can't just roam around the streets.* Her thoughts raced. Then a clear one caught hold. *I know, I'll call Ted. I'll ask him to help me, at least maybe he'll find me a place to stay.*

Then she remembered something Suzanne had said. Ted knew that Roarke was going to divorce me! Not only had he kept their separation a secret from me, but now this. Ted had convinced her in his office that he hadn't wanted to tell her of her separation from Roarke because she needed him or someone to take care of her. But to keep this a secret from her was inexcusable. He said he was her friend! With friends like Suzanne and Ted she certainly had her share of enemies.

Sara's mind felt like putty; her instinct to run took over, and she ran around the corner of the building and stopped short. Gasping in alarm, she saw Roarke entering the lobby. She ran back around the side of the building, breathing hard and, her heart pounding in her throat, waiting in rigid anticipation to hear Roarke's voice call her name. She didn't know how long she stood there, but when she knew that Roarke hadn't seen her, she started to run.

Running blindly, unaware of the curious stares of passers-by, she ran until she could run no more. Convulsively taking deep, panting breaths, she slowly became aware of where she was for the first time. She was standing in the Mall between the Lincoln Memorial and the Washington Monument and the reflecting pool was in front of her. Somehow she knew there were benches somewhere a little farther ahead where she could sit down, rest, and collect her thoughts. She didn't know how she knew about the benches; she just knew she had to reach one before she fell down.

She found a bench and practically collapsed on it. People walked by her, but no one paid any attention to her. Letting the pent-up tears fall, she sobbed silently. When she could cry no more and took notice of her surroundings again, there were very few people in the vicinity. She was practically alone. Alone . . . the word rang out in her head. She was alone, she had no one, no one who really cared about her. No one who gave a damn about her happiness. The only person in her life whom she loved thought of her as a burdensome obligation.

Sara saw a policeman walking in her direction and panic gripped her once again. Quickly she stood and tried to walk casually in the direction of the Washington Monument. She held her breath as she passed the officer, afraid that Roarke had alerted the police she was missing. But when he passed her without even looking in her direction, she let out her breath with a sigh.

Desperately trying to hang on to some coherent thoughts, she knew she must do something; she couldn't wander the streets all night. She tried to think of anyone she could call for help that wouldn't tell Roarke, and the only person she could think of was Ted. Would he tell? *After all,* her thoughts ran rampant, *I am his patient and if I tell him not to call Roarke, he has to do as I say!* She knew she had to find a pay phone and call Ted and trust him. He was her only hope. If she didn't soon find a place to stay, the police would become curious and she'd be back where she started.

She didn't know where she was but hoped she hadn't gone back toward the apartment building. Roarke might be driving around looking for her, so she stepped out of the glow of the streetlight she was standing under.

It could be that Roarke wasn't looking for her. Maybe he was feeling relieved that she had gone out of his life so easily. Sara's heart lurched. *If only I didn't love him so much.*

Despite everything that had happened, her love was deep and all-consuming. She had to disappear out of Washington but, most of all, she had to disappear out of Roarke's life. That's the only way Roarke could be happy. With all the things that Suzanne had told her and the few things Roarke had said, some of the pieces were beginning to fit into her puzzle. The picture wasn't clear yet, there were still mammoth gaps, but what she did know showed her that she had practically ruined Roarke's life. Since she was released from the hospital, he must have made a very real attempt to mend their marriage, but the past could not be put to rest. It was all very real to him and the pain of all those years just couldn't be anesthetized by a few short months.

She knew she couldn't remember and was a different person from the other Sara, but she also knew she could never convince Roarke. "The only question is where and how do I disappear?" she whispered.

Sara walked and walked. She wasn't sure how long she had wandered around looking for a pay phone. Of the two she saw, one was in use and a policeman was standing near the other. She walked by the National Gallery of Art, avoiding the late-night people milling around. In front of her the Capitol building loomed over the city like a white picture glued on the dark sky behind it. She turned up another street, praying she'd find a phone.

Her head was spinning from exhaustion and she was having a difficult time controlling her panic. It had been hot when she left the house this morning, but the night was cool and she shivered slightly.

As she passed in front of some store windows, she glanced at her reflection. She saw a bedraggled, scared woman staring back at her. Her eyes were wide and almost vacant from terror and the strain of maintaining the steel control over her emotions.

What if someone stopped her to ask her if she needed help because she looked sick? What would she say to them? She must find a phone; she must get in touch with Ted and get off the streets. She dragged herself a little farther on and found a telephone that wasn't being used. It was under a streetlight and as Sara approached it she carefully looked around to make sure no one was watching her.

With a shaking hand she put the change in the slot and punched Ted's number. The phone on the other end started ringing. *Let him be there, please let him be there.* Sara mouthed the words silently. The phone kept ringing, but no one answered it. Sara let it ring and ring, hoping against hope that he was just coming in and would answer.

Devastated, she finally hung up the receiver and stared around blankly. The panic she had been holding under restraint for so long was uncontrollable; she was beyond reasonable thought. She walked blindly through the streets and wandered mindlessly for hours. When she was once more rational, dawn was streaking the city sky.

She knew she had spent a great deal of time in an all-night coffee shop and that she had even gone into a bus station for a little while, but it seemed like it happened in a dream. It had no reality for her. Nothing seemed real except her aching body and her fear.

Looking around, she saw a hotel across the street. She had to sleep. Taking her wallet out of her purse, she saw there was money inside—her weekly allowance from Roarke. She just hoped it was enough. Desperate, not caring anymore if Roarke found her or not, she went into the hotel and paid for a room. She didn't pay any attention to the curious stares or that the night manager hesitated to give her a room until she had told him her name. She just took the proffered key and made her way to the elevator. Fumbling with the key in the lock, she got the door open, went inside, and locked the door behind her. Not bothering to take off her clothes, she collapsed on the bed and was immediately deeply asleep.

Her sleep was troubled and she thrashed around in the bed. She dreamed that Roarke and Suzanne were chasing her around the city. She ran and ran but couldn't find anyplace to hide. At one point she was running in slow motion, and when she turned around, she saw that Ted had joined the chase and they were all laughing and pointing their fingers at her. She would rouse awake and realize she was dreaming but fall back into a druglike sleep only to have the dream continue. Suddenly Sara woke with a start. Someone was pounding on the door.

"Sara, let me in!" It was Roarke and his voice sounded angry and hoarse. "Open this door and let me in." He kept pounding on the door until she thought he would break it in.

Sara shook her head, trying to make sure she was awake and that this was not a part of the nightmare she had been having. She was awake and the pounding continued. She was trapped. There was nowhere to run. She heard a key turn in the lock and panic rose in her throat.

When Roarke entered the room, Sara was lying in a heap on the floor, unconscious.

CHAPTER TEN

Sara blinked to clear her vision. Everything was blurred with a bright halo of light shimmering through the room. Where was she? Was she back in the hospital? Sensing someone nearby, she cautiously moved her head and through the murky haze made out Roarke's form sitting beside her. She closed her eyes quickly, hoping Roarke didn't notice she was awake.

"Sara, I know you're awake. Will you please open your eyes and look at me?" He sounded exhausted.

She opened her eyes again and stared at the ceiling. She couldn't look at him. Awareness was replacing her confusion along with the knowledge that she had been running away from him. Turning her head away, she gazed around and saw that he had brought her back to the apartment.

"Sara, why did you run away? You know you aren't in any condition to be roaming Washington alone." Roarke paused, waiting for her answer. "Damn it, Sara, will you look at me and answer my question!" Roarke's voice raised and it sounded hoarse.

She looked at Roarke through half-closed lids. His clothes were rumpled and a dark growth of beard marred the smooth, sleek skin. He looked as if he hadn't slept in days. The bloodshot eyes exposed his weariness and a faint crease between his brows lent his face an air of sadness and regret.

A deep sense of sympathy surged through her, but she steeled herself against it. It couldn't be those emotions she was seeing in his eyes. If it were, it was only because he was regretting that he had her as a burden again.

"Sara, please talk to me." His voice cracked roughly.

"How did you find me?" Sara asked weakly and turned her face away from him.

"The hotel manager called me. He was concerned when he saw how you looked. When you told him your name, he decided he'd better let me know you were there. Now, answer my question. Why did you run away?"

Emotionless, tired of struggling to hold on to her hopeless love, she knew she had to take the initiative and end this impasse. She knew she had to convince Roarke she was resolute in her decision to leave him.

"I don't want to be near you anymore. I don't want to share your life. All I want is a place to stay, by myself, for a little while. Once I decide what I want to do, where I want to go, I'll be out of your life forever. I think we made a wise decision two years ago when we separated. Even though I can't remember the reason for our separation, I know going back together is a mistake."

Glancing over her shoulder at Roarke, she thought she saw him wince. "If that's how you feel, then I'll make arrangements for you to be on your own." He rose stiffly from the bed and walked out of the room.

Sara rolled over, faced the window, and began to cry. She put her face into the pillow, hoping it would muffle the sound of her agony. She knew she had done the right thing, but the knowledge didn't ease the pain.

As her sobs eased she drifted into a dreamless sleep. When she woke again, the room was dark and the apartment was silent. Getting out of bed, her legs rubbery, she shakily tiptoed out of the bedroom into the living room and was surprised to see Roarke sitting in a chair. His elbows were resting on his knees and his face was lowered into the palms of his hands, the picture of exhaustion. Slowly he raised his head as he sensed she was standing there and looked up at her. If it were possible, he looked even more tired and haggard than he had earlier.

Roarke sighed audibly and in a strained voice said, "I've made arrangements for you to stay here. You can have Martha come and help you out when you need her or she can stay here with you, if you want. No one will bother you and you can make your plans however you want. The only thing I ask is that when you decide what you're going to do, I want to know. I want you to call me at my office and tell me your decision." He got up slowly and stood in front of Sara. She took the piece of paper he handed her and noticed there were a couple of telephone numbers written on it. He pointed to a number on the bottom of the paper. "This is my private number at the office if you need m . . . help. You can reach me without going through my secretary. Sara, I . . ." He reached out his hand as though to touch her face but changed his mind and dropped his hand to his side. He handed her the keys to the apartment. "Good-bye, Sara," he whispered, opened the door and walked out of the apartment without looking back.

She was alone, really alone. There was no more Roarke for her around any corner. She could stay here and not be disturbed. Suzanne must have hated giving up the apartment, even for the short time Sara would be using it. Sara wondered what Roarke had to promise her in order to persuade her to let Sara stay here. Maybe a speedy divorce and an early marriage to Suzanne was the inducement!

Walking into the kitchen, aimlessly looking around, she saw that Roarke had brewed a fresh pot of coffee. Opening the door of the refrigerator, she found a plate of sandwiches. His show of concern touched her, but she knew it was just one more sign of his feeling of responsibility.

Sara ate a sandwich and drank a cup of coffee. She wept as she ate and let the tears roll down her pale cheeks unchecked. When she thought of how silly she must look, eating and crying at the same time, she started giggling. It wasn't from amusement, it was because she felt on the edge of hysteria. She had to stop this nonsense! If she didn't, Roarke would probably somehow force her to move back to the house, reasoning with her that she was unfit to take care of herself.

She restlessly roamed the apartment, wondering what would make her feel better. When she flicked the light on in the bathroom, she stared at her image in the mirror. Horrified to see how filthy she was, she decided to soak in a bath. She turned on the tap and filled the tub with hot water. She stripped off her clothes and lowered her body into the soothing white bubbles and hot water and slowly relaxed.

Lying back in the steamy heat, she swished the bubbles up across her breasts and found her mind drifting back to Roarke's touch on her sensitive skin. Their lovemaking had been so spontaneous, so passionate. The warmth of the water rippling over her skin reminded her of the sun striking her body as they lay together under the blossom-laden trees. How could two people thrill to each other's touch and not be able to be happy out of bed? Somewhere the answer lay in the forgotten past.

The indisputable facts nudged the fantasy from her thoughts and she stood up, the rivulets of water running down her legs. She got out of the tub and wrapped herself in a towel. Why did their lives have to be this way? Her shoulders slumped from the burden of knowing she would never feel his closeness again, his body caressing hers. She would never know what it was like to be loved by him.

Sara rummaged through the closet, surprised by the clothes she found there and had found in the dresser drawers. They didn't seem to be the type Suzanne would wear. These clothes were more to Sara's taste. They were cool pastel colors, and the couple of times Sara had seen Suzanne, she had been wearing something flamboyant. With complete indifference she took a pink robe from a hanger and was putting it on when she noticed two cardboard boxes on the floor far back in the corner.

Curious, she plunged deeper into the closet and was startled to see her name printed on the boxes. She pulled and tugged and managed to get them into the living room. They must have been stored in the closet when Suzanne moved in, she thought.

Sara poured herself another cup of coffee and curled up on the sofa with her feet tucked under the pink robe, opened one of the boxes, and reached for some photos that were laying on top.

A few were pictures of her wedding. Roarke looked so young and so handsome and she looked like an ethereal child. Roarke wore a black tuxedo and a ruffled white shirt and she wore a long cream-colored gown and a wide-brimmed hat. The date printed on the back of the wedding pictures was June 24, 1974. They had been married over eight years and, with a pang, she realized their ninth wedding anniversary was only a few weeks away.

Running her hand lovingly over Roarke's handsome, smiling face, she laid the pictures on the sofa beside her. The next few photos could only be of her graduation from high school. She was in a cap and gown, standing between Roarke and a frail-looking, gray-haired lady that she knew was her grandmother. The date on this picture was May 1974. She had married Roarke when she was only eighteen years old. How long had she known him? *I must have been wildly in love with him to have married him as soon as I graduated from school,* she mused. *I didn't even give myself a chance to grow up!*

She studied her grandmother's face. The woman looked ill. Not only was she frail, but her face was drawn and pinched. There was a smile on the wrinkled face, but a look of pain seemed half-concealed in her eyes. Martha had told her that her grandmother had died about a year after she and Roarke had married. She wondered if her grandmother had been ill a long time.

Perplexed, she shook her head and dug deeper into the box. Her hand found a small book, and when she brought it out to the surface, she found she was holding a diary. Her heart pounded against her rib cage. Maybe this would hold some answers for her.

Sara flipped through the pages, reading entries at random,

musing over some of her day-to-day activities. As she read, several things became clear. She depended on Martha for parental love, and she had been jealous of Roarke's activities that took him away from her so much of the time. In the diary the excuse she had used for their increased fighting was that she loved him but he constantly treated her like a child. Toward the end of the diary, Sara read the pages more carefully. Suzanne's name seemed to be coming up more frequently.

That woman was here again today, looking for Roarke! She came on the pretext of dropping off some plans that her father wanted Roarke to see. The day Roarke accepted the contract on her father's new office complex was the day he gave her carte blanche to interfere in our lives. Suzanne has made it quite clear over the past several months that she thinks I'm a spoiled brat and not good enough for Roarke. Today when she demanded to see Roarke, and I told her he wasn't home, she became nasty. She told me she was going to take Roarke away from me and that there wasn't a thing I can do to stop her. I can't warn Roarke, he'll think I'm just behaving childishly again. I wish I knew how to get Suzanne out of our lives.

The last entry was dated about two years ago and was three pages long.

Today I went to Roarke's office to meet him for lunch. Roarke wasn't there, so I waited in his private office rather than sit in the reception room. I noticed that a small file cabinet in the back corner of the office had the drawer opened partway. When I went to close it, my eye caught the name on a file folder that was pulled up above the others. It was my name! Curious, I took the folder out and opened it and found it was filled with papers and newspaper clippings.

There were legal papers and some letters. One letter I read was from my grandma to Roarke, who was in London at the time. It was dated the year I was a senior in high school. She told Roarke she was dying and asked if he would take care of me afterward. A later letter from Grandma was filled with gratitude that Roarke had consented to take over my guardianship. Consented! Guardianship!

He doesn't love me, he never loved me! He married me to solve Grandma's problem. I'm going to leave him. I won't force him to go through this farce anymore. This "problem" is going to solve itself!

Sara threw the diary across the room and whimpered in agony. She remembered all of it! She knew who she was, where she'd been. All the joy, all the pain were hers once more. In her mind she could see her parents' faces and she could see the house she had lived in with Grandma. She could remember her happiness when Roarke started dating her. She had always had a crush on him. The first time she had gone out with him, she had felt so flattered. The day of her marriage had been the happiest day in her life, but she was still in awe of Roarke.

Now she understood so many things. She had worshipped Roarke as a god; she hadn't loved him like a man. When he didn't . . . or couldn't . . . live up to her expectation of how a god should behave, she had felt somehow cheated.

She had accused him of being unfaithful because she was insecure. Her immature reasoning was such that why should he want to remain faithful to her when there were so many beautiful women just waiting for Roarke to notice them? Now she knew that she instigated the fights with Roarke because, when they were fighting, she had his undivided attention. When he was angry with her, he wasn't thinking about work or anything else—he was thinking only of her.

Sara realized now that all the antics she had performed were to get Roarke's attention. Roarke had been busy building his business; he didn't have as much time for Sara as she thought he should have, so she did outrageous things to make him notice her.

Finding the letters in Roarke's office had been a terrible shock, the final blow. When Roarke had walked into his office with Suzanne in tow, Sara's hurt and confusion turned to fury. She had screamed at them, accusing them of everything she could think of.

She had waved one of her grandmother's letters in his face. "How dare you, you lying cheat, how dare you pull this on me. Our entire marriage has been a farce. This is the last straw!" she screamed.

Roarke grabbed her wrist and his fingers bit into her flesh. "What in the hell are you talking about, Sara? What is this you have in your hand?" He grabbed at the letter with his other hand and tore it from her grasp.

"Roarke, I've often wondered why you married me, and now I know. You did it because you promised my grandmother to take care of me. And how long do you think I'd be so stupid to believe you married me for love, not the business? What better way to gain control of the business than to marry your dead partner's daughter? I'd say I've been stupid long enough. I've lived in ignorance for all these years but no longer."

"Sara, for God's sake listen to me! I love you, always have—"

Turning on her heel, Sara stomped to the office door and with her hand on the knob, she turned, her wrath glittering in her amber eyes, turning them to golden sparks of light. "I'm leaving you, Roarke. When you get home, I won't be there, and there will be no reconciliation this time, believe me." The glittering cold gold eyes swept over Suzanne. "You don't need me anyway. You have your new playmate." She opened the door and swept through the opening but not before she caught the sight of Suzanne's face with a knowing smile on it, the smile telling Sara that Suzanne knew she was destroying herself with her own words.

* * *

After she moved into their apartment in Washington, D.C., she spent a lot of time alone, trying to relieve her misery with her painting. But when she was invited to a party, she was escorted by a different man each time, she made sure of that. Sara had hoped that by flaunting her numerous escorts she would rouse Roarke's jealousy. However, she didn't become involved with any of them, even though several had fallen in love with her.

Her separation from Roarke had given her time to think about him and her feelings for him. She loved Roarke and her love was going through a miraculous change. She was beginning to grow up. The time she spent alone was spent examining herself, getting to know herself. She was beginning to love Roarke with a new maturity, learning that real love, true love, was not selfish, was not taking all, giving nothing in return. Real love, mature love was giving, sharing, wanting the other person's happiness as much as your own, if not more. She had lain awake many nights and cried, tempted to call Roarke, to beg his forgiveness, to tell him she had at last grown up. She ached to tell him how much she loved him, ached with a longing for him that was overwhelming. But the letter she had seen in his office would come back into her mind and she just couldn't call him. She couldn't become his responsibility, his obligation, again.

Wearily Sara stood up, went into the bathroom, and looked into the mirror. She was whole again. Physically she was still the same, but the lost look was gone from her eyes, replaced by recognition. What couldn't be reflected in the mirror was the way she felt. She knew she was no longer the immature young girl Roarke had known.

Sara's face flamed in humiliation, remembering the stupid, childish things she had done to Roarke. Many nights when Roarke had done something that didn't please her, she had slept in the guest room with the door locked. This little ploy had worked for a while, but Roarke soon tired of that game. Later, on the nights she had spent in the guest room, Roarke had slammed out of the house and stayed out all night.

It soon became a vicious circle that Sara didn't know how to break. She started playing more games. She had flowers sent to the house with unsigned cards in them, hoping Roarke would assume they were from some unnamed admirer. Their fighting increased and rarely did they have any peace between them. It culminated that day in Roarke's office when she read the letters in the file.

Sara realized she was gripping the edge of the bathroom basin so hard that her hands were numb. Her neck was hurting from holding her head rigidly as she gazed into the mirror, hypnotized by memories that were flowing like a torrent through her brain.

She walked out of the bathroom dejectedly and threw herself onto the bed. Reaching out, she turned off the bedside light and stared into the dark space of the room. Memories flowed unchecked, and some of them were agonizing. She wondered how Roarke had put up with her juvenile behavior for so long. *But, she thought, that just proves he really didn't love me. If he had loved me, he would have tried to understand me and help me grow up but instead, when we weren't fighting, he indulged my every whim.*

If he would have just once treated me like an adult, maybe I would have responded like one. The only time he did respond to me as a woman was when we were in bed. If only once he would have told me to grow up, that he needed me as a woman, it might have made a difference. Her hands flew over her eyes. But would it have?

She could see their marriage was doomed from the beginning. She had worshipped him like a hero and he had been her baby-sitter. Instead of changing as they grew older, they had viewed each other as the same undeveloped person they had married, so the marriage never matured. Roarke almost acted as though she were too stupid to understand the intricacies of his business, so he never shared any of his problems with her, and she had felt left out. They had trapped each other in the mold that had formed them years before.

Sara rolled onto her stomach and put her hands over the edge of the bed. She unconsciously ran her fingers through the thick carpeting. Roarke had seen their marriage as a solution to a problem and an answer that had soothed a dying woman.

Poor Grandma. I wonder if she knows what has happened to her happy solution, Sara thought. Her grandmother had never told Sara that she was dying, although she had known her grandmother was ill. Sara would ask her repeatedly what was wrong, and she would tell her that it was an old complaint that bothered her occasionally. Sara was always reassured by that answer, therefore she was stricken and heartbroken when her grandmother died.

Roarke had been very gentle and loving with her. He stayed by her side throughout the funeral. After the services they'd driven to Annapolis and Sara had immediately fallen in love with its old-world charm and beauty. Sara smiled to herself in the dark, thinking of how she and Roarke had loved Annapolis and the fun they had had there.

On their second anniversary Roarke took a long weekend and they had gone to Annapolis to celebrate. When they arrived, they had driven passed the hotel where they usually stayed. Sara had been surprised and protested, but her protests died in her throat when he had presented her with the keys to the town house. "Happy anniversary, Sara, this is yours, the deed is in your name. It's your retreat when the world becomes too much." He had placed the keys in her hand.

They had spent the night there in sleeping bags. The next day they had gone shopping and she selected all the furniture for her new home. It was really hers! She had laughed and clapped her hands together, delighted that she had her own hideaway, like a child with a new dollhouse. Sometimes when Roarke would go

158

away on a business trip, Sara would go to Annapolis by herself. At night she sat on the balcony off her bedroom and watched the lights of the distant boats bobbing out on the bay. She had made the town house her home away from home.

"That's were I'll stay," Sara said, sitting up in bed. "I'll go to Annapolis." She chuckled to herself when she remembered she had been going to do that before she had regained her memory. But the big difference now was that she could remember the address.

She didn't have to worry about money, her savings account was very healthy, so she could afford the upkeep on her own. Her father and Roarke's father had been partners in the construction company, and when her father had been killed, she had inherited his share, put into a trust for her to be administered by her grandmother. As the business had grown through Roarke's expert leadership after his father had died, so had her personal wealth.

At one time she had offered to sign over her share of the business to him, but Roarke wouldn't hear of it. The only thing he would let her do was give him her power of attorney to make all the business decisions, so she still received her share of the profits.

She would have to figure out how she could get to Annapolis. She was still a little fuzzy about the accident, but from what she could remember and from what Roarke had told her, her car had been totally demolished.

"I could rent a car," Sara said out loud again. Her voice echoed around the room and sounded hollow in the empty apartment.

Tears spilled over her lashes again. She didn't think it was possible that she could cry anymore, but she did. She had thought when she regained her memory that she would be whole once more, but without Roarke in her life, she would never be whole, she loved him completely.

The accident had changed her. It had been the impact that burst her from her cocoon, turning her from a child into a woman—a woman who knew she could love only one man—a man she could never have, a man who would never know that his childlike bride had finally grown up.

CHAPTER ELEVEN

By the time dawn was streaking the sky, she had mentally gone over her entire life with Roarke several times. One of her last thoughts before she drifted off into a fitful sleep was that she had been so stupid, but he hadn't been much smarter. They were really both to blame for their failed marriage, just as Roarke had said.

When she woke up, it was late and her head felt thick and her eyes were heavy-lidded and swollen. She groped her way to the kitchen and made some coffee, and when it finished brewing, she sat in the living room waiting for it to revive her. But the coffee didn't do its usual job, and she thought a shower might help her feel better.

After her shower she went to the closet, wondering what she could find to wear temporarily. She'd have to return to the house and get some of her own clothes. She opened the closet door and was dumbfounded. These were her clothes! None of the clothes in the closet were Suzanne's. Suzanne had lied to her! Suzanne wasn't living here, all these clothes were her very own.

Sara was angry. How could Roarke love someone like Suzanne? Even when she couldn't remember Suzanne, there was something malignant about her. Was Roarke so completely blind where women were concerned?

As she dressed in corded jeans and a western shirt, she continued to mumble to herself about Roarke's stupidity. She was making the bed when she heard the doorbell ring. "Now, who

161

in the world could that be?" she muttered to herself as she stalked to the door to answer it. *I hope it's Suzanne! If it is, I'm not going to let her know I have my memory back. I'll string her along until she gives me the right opening and then let her have it,* she resolved to herself.

Sara opened the door, prepared to do battle but was surprised to see it was Roarke's body filling the entire door frame. He looked extremely tired, his face was drawn, and his eyes were puffy. Sara wondered why he looked so bad. Could he have been out all night celebrating?

"May I come in?" he asked, his voice low and gravelly.

Sara stood aside and motioned for him to come in. She didn't know what to say and a terrible sense of loss was clutching at her.

Roarke looked around at the open boxes and the pictures spread out all over the sofa. He sat down and picked up a picture that was lying beside him. "What made you decide to look through all this?" he inquired, holding the picture up so she could see it.

"I saw those boxes with my name on them in the closet and I dragged them out here to see what they were." Sara shrugged her shoulders.

"Did it help?" he asked tonelessly. Sara didn't detect the old sarcasm in his voice she had half-expected.

Sighing, she sat in a chair across from him. "Yes, as a matter of fact it did. I was reading through an old diary of mine and I've remembered . . . everything. After all this time I thought I'd never remember, but all it took was going through those boxes," Sara pointed to the things scattered around the living room.

"You remember everything?" He seemed to choke on the question.

Sara watched his face intently. It blanched white and then color crept up from his neck. There was no happiness, no love, nothing that would give her any hope of being able to straighten out this mess that they called their marriage. All her thoughts, all her conclusions were accurate. He didn't love her. Their marriage had been to make a dying old woman happy and consolidate a business.

Sara got up and started pacing the room. "Yes, I've remembered all of it, Roarke, all of it!" She couldn't look at him, she was afraid he would read the lie in her eyes. He wouldn't end this farce so she had to, and it was breaking her heart.

"I've decided to go to Annapolis. The place is mine and I need somewhere to stay. I have to make a new life for myself. I want a divorce. I don't want to be trapped in this marriage any longer." Sara glanced at him out of the corner of an eye and thought she could see his hands shaking. Was her news about wanting a divorce such a relief to him that he was having trouble controlling his excitement? Was he that much in love with Suzanne? Did the prospect of being able to marry her soon make him shake in anticipation? She had to quit torturing herself. This is the way things are between them and she would have to accept it.

"I see." He took a cigarette out of his shirt pocket and fumbled with his lighter. "You don't have a car; how do you plan to get to Annapolis?" Roarke took a deep drag on his cigarette and blew the smoke out in a long stream. He ran his hand nervously through his dark hair. His skin was ashen-colored and taut over his high cheekbones and his face seemed more angular than usual.

She cleared her throat. "I plan to rent a car. After I'm settled in, I'll buy one. Although I guess I'll have to make several trips to move all my clothing and painting equipment." She sat down again, still keeping her distance from Roarke.

Roarke stood up, stubbed out his cigarette in an ashtray, and walked over to her. "Are you sure this is how you want it?"

Sara nodded her head; she couldn't speak. She knew if she tried, her resolve would weaken and she'd tell Roarke how much she didn't want to leave him, how much she loved him.

"I'll drive you to Annapolis. I'll also contact someone to move you. I'll have Martha pack your things at the house. Just let me

163

know when you're ready to leave." His last words were whispered. He turned abruptly and left the apartment, closing the door carefully but firmly behind him.

Sara was emotionally exhausted. Her hurt went so deep, no tears could ease it. He couldn't wait for her to be out of his life. Even moving her own things was too slow to satisfy him. Roarke's seeming eagerness to be rid of her and all her possessions hurt her beyond anything he had done to her so far. Now that she had her memory back, he couldn't wait to unburden himself of the responsibility he felt for her. Finally he would be free of her, and he couldn't wait.

She wandered around the apartment for hours, thinking about Roarke, their marriage, and her love for him. She touched well-loved things and remembered how and where she had bought them or when Roarke had given them to her. She lavished the photos of Roarke with her unrequited love. Walking by the door to her studio, she suddenly remembered it was locked and got the key from the dresser drawer. Unlocking the door, she moved among her beloved paintings. They were hanging all over the walls and stacked against them. Roarke and Annapolis were her favorite subjects. Roarke's face was everywhere. She remembered after she left him, on the nights when she couldn't sleep, she would get out of bed and paint for hours, cursing the strokes that weren't right, the colors that muddied, and not cursing her life. It had absorbed her, her painting. It had kept her sane, kept her functioning.

She wasn't aware of how much time had passed during her reminiscences of the past until she looked out the window and realized it was getting dark. Sara knew she needed a positive plan of action. Thinking of the past would not do her any good. Now that she could remember, she must let the past go. She was a complete person once more and, like anyone else, dwelling on the past would not change anything that had happened.

Sara laughed to herself mirthlessly at this ironic change in her life. For months she had lived in despair because she couldn't remember, and now that she had remembered, she knew she must put it all behind her.

Burning tears filled her eyes and threatened the composed facade she was desperately trying to hide behind. She angrily wiped the tears from her face. There would be time for tears later. She had to take action and make arrangements to get out of Roarke's life as fast as she could.

She decided to call Roarke and ask him if he could take her to Annapolis tomorrow. She would pack a few suitcases and be ready to leave by morning. The sooner she could get away from him, the sooner she could heal her smashed life.

Now that she had made her decision, she wanted to tell Roarke and get it over with quickly. She called everywhere she could think of, but no one had seen Roarke or heard from him in the past few hours. He seemed to have disappeared completely. It dawned on her that Roarke was probably at Suzanne's, but she refused to call him there. She left messages on his office recorder and with Bradley. Now she'd just have to wait for him to return her call.

Sara curled up on the sofa, but her mind kept going back to Roarke. Was he in Suzanne's arms? Was he excitedly telling her that they could get married now because Sara had agreed to a divorce? Were they in bed, making love?

"So what!" Sara said aloud. "If they are in bed, it has nothing to do with me anymore." The sound of her voice echoed around the silent room long after her words faded into oblivion. She bolted off the sofa and stood in the middle of the room, her tautly drawn nerves making it impossible for her to sit still.

She looked at the diary and the pictures still scattered around the room and decided to finish going through them. It would cause her excruciating pain, but once she had finished, she could seal both boxes and put them away. She hoped she could as easily seal up the past as she could the boxes.

There were newspaper clippings about charity events and functions they had attended. Their lives had been one of social togetherness and smiles for the society pages, but their private life the last several years of their marriage had been one of arguments, accusations, and bitterness.

The ringing of the doorbell startled her. Glancing at the clock on the table, she wondered who could possibly be visiting at this time of night! She froze before she got to the door. What if it were Roarke again, what would she do? She just couldn't face him right now! Her determination would crumble if she had to face him one more time today. She stood in front of the door, wringing her hands with indecision.

If it were Roarke, he was persistent. The constant ringing was grating on her nerves. She'd have to answer it; he wasn't going to go away. Taking a deep breath, Sara forced herself to open the door. The breath she'd been holding escaped from her in a rush. Roarke wasn't standing in the open doorway—it was Suzanne.

Before Sara could utter a word, Suzanne brushed passed her and marched into the living room. She held the door open, half-expecting Roarke to be close behind Suzanne but, looking up and down the hallway, she didn't see him anywhere. Closing the door slowly, she wondered what Suzanne wanted. She had just about had it, and the amazing amount of gall this woman possessed was unbelievable.

Striding back into the living room, Sara said impatiently, "What do you want, Suzanne?" *Of all the people to have to bother me at this time!* Sara's thoughts exploded. She couldn't understand why Suzanne was here, but she really didn't care. She was tired of Suzanne and all her conniving. All Sara wanted to do was get her out of the apartment and out of her life.

"I want to know what you think you're doing." Suzanne's voice was full of contempt and her mouth was curled in a sneer. She stood in the middle of the living room, hands on hips, and her face suffused with anger and hatred.

Sara shuddered. "I don't understand what you're talking about, and I really don't care to know. I have nothing to say to you. Would you please just leave," Sara said emphatically, pointing to the front door.

"I'm not going anywhere until you tell me what you said to Roarke," Suzanne said just as emphatically, and sat down in one of the chairs.

Resigned to the inevitable, Sara also sat down. Obviously she couldn't forceably throw her out, so she'd have to listen to her. Sara did notice though that Suzanne wasn't her usual cool, assured self. As a matter of fact, as Sara looked at her more closely, there was something decidedly wrong. She was usually perfectly made up, coiffed, and dressed, but tonight, she had a neglected, wild look. What did she do, rush right over here from a warm bed after making love with Roarke to rub salt in Sara's wounds? Sara was disgusted.

Suzanne's eyes glittered and her agitation was clear as she took out a cigarette and it fell on the floor. Fumbling with the pack, she pulled out another one, ignoring the one that had fallen.

With cold anger Sara watched as Suzanne attempted to regain her composure. *She* was now in command of the situation, not this unkempt woman. Sara smiled inwardly.

"I want to know what you said to Roarke when he was here this afternoon," Suzanne demanded again.

"And I told you before, I don't know what you're talking about. I said a lot of things to Roarke this afternoon. If you knew he was here, you must know what we discussed," Sara stated coolly. She wouldn't let herself be baited into giving Suzanne any information.

Suzanne sat back into the chair, relaxing a little as she inhaled deeply on her cigarette. "All right, Sara, I'm not going to waste any more time or words on you. If you think you've won, you're sadly mistaken." Suzanne was purring now, restraining her earlier agitation.

Watching Suzanne was amazing. She was a completely different person from the woman who had walked into the apartment. Her outward appearance was still the same, but now she was a cat on the prowl—smooth and confident. Sara decided to remain silent because, she mused, two could play the same game.

"Roarke didn't give me a blow-by-blow account of what went on here, but he did let me know that you have once more played on his sympathy for you. Do you think you can hold on to a man very long with pity?" Suzanne smiled smugly at Sara. "You can't, you know. Pity can become a very boring emotion." Suzanne paused, waiting for Sara to say something, and when she didn't, she became plainly irritated again.

"Roarke and I may be finished for the time being, but it's not permanent. You can count on that! You may have won him back temporarily through pity, but you won't be able to keep him through pity. He'll get tired of pampering you and long for a real woman, and that real woman will be me!" Suzanne smiled, a look of satisfaction giving her back her appearance of superiority.

Sara stood up. "If that's all you have to say, you may leave now. What is between Roarke and me is none of your business." Sara was furious but pretended to be weary of this conversation. She was completely mystified; she had no idea what Suzanne was talking about, but she would not give her the satisfaction of asking for an explanation.

Shock passed over Suzanne's face and then rage, a rage Suzanne barely concealed. It frightened Sara, but she knew not to show the fear she felt. She was determined not to let Suzanne get the upper hand.

Suzanne rose from the chair but didn't move toward the door. She just stood rigidly in front of Sara. "I won't let you have Roarke," she snarled. "I've cultivated this relationship for two long years and I won't give him up to some silly woman who's never grown up. You can never give him what I can. I understand his business and I'm an excellent hostess. I have connections in society and I can introduce him to all the right people," Suzanne pointed out imperiously.

"What about love?" Sara asked simply, in a quiet voice.

"Love!" Suzanne spat out. "You've got to be kidding. What

168

does love have to do with anything? It's mutual usefulness that keeps a marriage viable, not love. You are a child, Sara. Love!" Suzanne's sarcastic laughter filled the room.

"No, Suzanne, I am not a child," Sara said calmly and quietly. "In fact, I've grown up quite a bit, especially the last few hours. I know what game you're playing, Suzanne, and I've known for years."

Suzanne gaped at Sara incredulously. "You . . . you remember?"

"Didn't you tell me I didn't have amnesia, Suzanne? Didn't you sit right there"—Sara pointed to the chair—"and tell me you didn't believe I had amnesia and was playing a childish game on Roarke?"

"But . . . but you did have amnesia! I knew when I walked in on you and Roarke in the study that night that you didn't remember me. I knew, because you hated me so much you would have never been able to cover that hatred. I used that hatred to get Roarke and I used your amnesia to try to get rid of you."

"Yes, you used, Suzanne. But no more. I feel sorry for you. I really do if all the pleasure you derive from life is trying to hurt people and use them, I feel really sorry for you. Now, will you please leave!" Sara demanded.

Suzanne sauntered lazily to the door. Her green eyes were slits and smoldered with hatred. With her hand on the knob, she turned to Sara. "Sorry? You feel sorry for me? Don't waste that emotion on me. You're going to need it for yourself. You know, Sara, I'm almost convinced that you and Roarke deserve each other. When he called me this afternoon and told me to stay out of his life, I was furious. He said he would never marry me because he didn't love me." Suzanne's laughter sounded shrill in Sara's ears. "I think I'll leave you two to each other. Let's see how long it takes Roarke to get tired of love and you. He'll be glad to come back to me. Then you'll have lots of time to feel sorry." Suzanne slammed the door behind her.

Sara was utterly puzzled. Did Roarke really call Suzanne and tell her they were finished? He must have; Suzanne's anger was certainly real enough. Why would he do that if he had been planning to marry her? And why would she assume he was coming back to me? Drained, she walked into her bedroom, undressed, and slipped under the covers. Thinking back to the time of Suzanne's intrusion into their lives, it had been Suzanne who had done all the chasing. She would come to the house on some pretext of discussing a blueprint or some alteration she and her father had decided upon.

Sara had become so sick of this that she had finally ordered Bradley to tell Suzanne no one was home when she would unexpectedly appear on their doorstep.

But Suzanne did not give up. She started turning up constantly at Roarke's office. She had insisted on lunch and dinner meetings. Sara had raised so much hell about that that Roarke had eliminated as many of the meetings as he could.

Once Sara had left Roarke, Suzanne became his occasional date. Sara couldn't really remember hearing of him going out with anyone else. Had he been using Suzanne to give Sara a good reason to end the marriage? Did he want her to end the marriage so he wouldn't feel responsible for having ended it himself?

Sara could feel the turmoil beginning to churn inside her again. She'd never get to sleep if she continued thinking this way. She had to settle herself. She had made a decision and she would stick to it. If Roarke had broken off with Suzanne, he must have had his reasons. Obviously Roarke didn't want to start his single life cluttered with anyone from his past.

Rolling and tossing, she tried to clear her mind of all her troubled thoughts, but she was happy that Suzanne wouldn't be part of Roarke's life anymore. Sara loved him enough to want him to be happy, and she knew he could never be happy with Suzanne.

Waking suddenly to what she thought was the doorbell ringing, she realized it was the telephone. She groped around on her nightstand for the receiver. "Hello," she said groggily into the phone when she managed to get it to her ear.

"Sara, it's Roarke. I just got your message that you called and wanted to talk with me. What do you want?"

Even in her sleep-drugged mind, Roarke sounded tired. "I wanted to ask you if you could take me to Annapolis in the morning." Sara sat up in bed, suddenly wide-awake.

"It will have to wait until evening. I have several things I must do. Will seven thirty be all right?" he asked. Roarke was short and to the point. He sounded impatient, as though he wanted to end the conversation quickly.

"Yes . . . yes, that's fine. It will give me time to get some of my things together that I want to take with me."

Before Sara could say another word, the line went dead. Roarke had hung up. She sighed and slipped back under the covers. What time is it anyway? she thought. Her room was still in darkness. Turning on the light, she looked at her alarm clock. It was four o'clock in the morning! What was he doing calling her at this hour? Couldn't he have waited until later in the morning? Sara put the pillow over her head and tried to fall back asleep.

A few hours later Sara slowly climbed out of bed. She couldn't fall back to sleep after Roarke's phone call. Her whirling brain had kept her rolling and sleepless. About seven o'clock she decided that the mattress was full of rocks and, stumbling zombie-like into the kitchen, she made coffee. After several cups she decided she was beyond hope; she couldn't go back to sleep and she seemed doomed to spend the rest of the day half-awake.

Locating her suitcases in the hall closet, she decided to pack, maybe some kind of activity would help her feel better. Each thing she packed, each suitcase completed and standing by the front door took her one more step away from the man she loved.

Later in the morning as she lay on the sofa, she tried to imagine what her life would be like if Roarke had only loved her. Her fantasy helped her drift partly to sleep when she heard a

171

sharp knock on the door, then the sound of a key being inserted into the lock. Startled, Sara sat up.

Roarke nearly tripped over her suitcases that were on the floor. Once he regained his balance, he came striding into the living room. "So you're packed and ready to leave," he observed as he sat down. "I'm hungry. We'll walk to the restaurant across the street and have some lunch before we start for Annapolis." He pulled a cigarette from his shirt pocket.

Sara's head was spinning. "Wait a minute, what are you doing here? I thought you wouldn't be here until later this evening. And what in the world possessed you to call me at four this morning?" Sara was furious. He had called her in the middle of the night, waking her up, and now he was sitting here like her lord and master ordering her around. What was his hurry?

Roarke shrugged his shoulders. "I've changed my plans. I'm going away, and this is the only time I can drive you to Annapolis. I called you at four this morning because you had left so many messages, I thought there was something wrong."

"You're going away?" Sara couldn't keep from asking. She had a strange sinking sensation in the pit of her stomach.

"Yes, I'm going to the West Coast for several months. I've got to oversee the starting construction on the resort community contract I told you about. It's an important job and I want to give it my personal attention. I'll be leaving in a few days and I have quite a few arrangements to make." He drew heavily on his cigarette and, to Sara, he seemed extremely disturbed. He got up and walked around the room, his restlessness cutting her to the quick.

Sara couldn't think of anything to say. The extent of her hurt and the deep disappointment at the news of his going away made her realize with a jolt that she had been nursing a secret hope that in some way they could still work things out.

Sara watched Roarke; his impatience was transmitting itself to her with his every move. *He's in such a hurry to shed these last eight years and his responsibility for me that it makes me sick at*

172

heart. Her heart was breaking into a thousand pieces and no one would ever be able to find them all to put them back together. Her wretchedness rose in her throat and threatened to choke off her breathing. Tears were burning behind her eyes.

She sat in her chair, trying to keep herself under control. Her hands were balled into fists and she dug her nails into the palms of her hands trying to focus her mind on that pain instead of the pain inside her. No, this pain wasn't just inside her, this pain seared her very soul. A life without Roarke was inconceivable, but he had made it clear over and over that he didn't want her.

Sara slowly rose from the chair. "I'm going into my room and get the rest of my things." Her voice sounded steady, which surprised her. She must not expose her pain to him. She could fall apart when she was alone in Annapolis. *I will not let him see what this is doing to me,* she thought as she stood in the middle of her bedroom. *I don't want him to pity me and I certainly don't want to take advantage of his feeling that he's responsible for me.* She couldn't understand why he would feel so responsible, but he did and she would not use this to try to get him back.

"Sara, could you hurry, please?"

Roarke's voice broke through her tormented thoughts. Roarke was standing beside her with a peculiar look on his face.

"I'm sorry, Roarke, what did you say?" Sara mindlessly moved to the dresser, opening drawers and closing them again without any purpose except to keep her trembling hands busy and so she wouldn't have to look directly at him.

"I said, are you ready to leave? I have a lot of things I have to do today and it's at least a couple of hours drive to Annapolis and back." He seemed as reluctant to look at Sara as she was to meet his eyes. He walked over to the window but moved quickly back to the door and left the bedroom. It seemed as though he couldn't stand still.

We're two strangers. Anyone seeing us would never believe we've been married for so long, Sara thought. Her misery was absolute. His question finally penetrated her befogged brain. "I'll be ready to leave in a few minutes," she called out to him, her voice sounding stilted in her ears. She glanced around the room to see that nothing remained behind.

How much easier this would be if I could just forget the past and start anew! Sara realized what she had just thought. She started laughing. For months she had been unable to remember the past and she had nearly driven herself insane trying to remember it. Now she was wishing she could forget all of it. Her laughter rose hysterically.

CHAPTER TWELVE

"Sara! Sara, stop it right now!"

The sting of his hand across her cheek shocked her. She slapped her hand to her mouth and tried to stop her mounting hysteria. Shaking her roughly, Roarke continued to yell her name. Her cheeks were wet with tears and suddenly she sagged from overpowering weakness. Against her will her body slumped onto Roarke's powerful chest. His arms circled around her and he picked her up and gently carried her over to the bed, murmuring soothing words.

A few moments later she felt a cold cloth on her forehead. Opening her eyes, she met Roarke's solemn gaze. "Are you all right? What happened?" With a worried expression he tenderly placed his hand along her cheek and softly stroked it in an effort to comfort her.

"I don't know what happened but I . . . I think I'm all right." Sara took the cold cloth from her head and inched her body up against the headboard of the bed, trying to escape his disturbing touch.

Roarke reached over and took the cloth from her hand. "I was just checking that everything was secured in the apartment when I heard you laughing. At first I thought you were on the phone, but when I heard your laughter changing and you were sounding hysterical, I came in here to find out what was wrong. You didn't even know I was here! I tried to talk to you, but you didn't seem to hear me. I'm sorry I had to slap you, but I didn't know what else to do. I'm . . . I'm so sorry, Sara." His voice was anguished and his eyes were so pained that she couldn't look away.

Then Sara saw something more in his eyes than pain. Could it be she was still in the grip of her hysteria? That could be the only explanation for what she thought she saw. Rubbing her hands roughly over her eyes, she blinked, trying to focus clearly on Roarke's face. The tone of his voice, the look in his eyes, the unguarded expression on his face, were telling her something that made her spirit soar with hope. This was not the look of a man who saw her as a responsibility or a burden he wanted to shed. She reached out a trembling hand and touched his cheek. It was wet! Looking at her damp fingers, she was puzzled. Were his cheeks wet from her tears or could it be from his tears? "Roarke," she whispered, his name sounding more like a moan.

"Sara . . . my sweet Sara." He pulled her roughly against his chest and held her so tightly it was as if he were sure she'd try to escape him again.

Sara clung to him desperately, afraid to hope what this might mean, yet not wanting to let go of this moment no matter what his meaning. "Roarke, I love you." Her voice was muffled against his shirt and she was afraid he had heard her but at the same time afraid that he hadn't.

"What did you say?" he demanded, beseeching her to repeat it, holding her away from him so he could look into her eyes.

"I said, I love you, Roarke. There's no sense denying it anymore." Sara hung her head, fearful of seeing the possible rejection in his eyes.

"Don't play games with me, Sara, I can't stand anymore. I've waited so long for you to say those words and really know what they mean, but if this is a game, it will destroy me." His voice hardened and his hands that were holding on to her shoulders bit into her flesh.

"Playing games. My God, Roarke, I'm not playing games. When I woke up in the hospital not knowing who I was or who you were, I was so scared. I couldn't remember anything of our

176

past, but I fell in love with you all over again. With you, as you are now. I'm not playing games." She hung her head. "Now let me go and I'll finish packing." Sara shifted away from him, but he didn't loosen his grasp on her shoulders. If anything, his hold on her tightened.

"Sara, you don't know what you're saying, do you? You're upset for some reason and you're just clinging to me because I'm familiar. Once you're on your own in Annapolis and have some time to think, you'll feel differently." He released her shoulders abruptly and she fell back against the headboard.

She rolled away from him and jumped off the bed, standing defiantly in front of Roarke. "How dare you tell me what or how I feel. Since when did I need any psychiatric advice from you? You've always patronized me or treated me like a child. I am not a child, I am a woman!" Her eyes were on fire and her breasts heaved with her anger and indignation.

Roarke sat motionless on the edge of the bed, his eyes wide with shock. His hands gripped the edge of the mattress and the bedspread was crushed beneath his clenched fists.

Sara was beyond caution or caring. She had had enough of this charade they played, each one treading carefully around the other, never saying what they really felt, just what they thought the other one wanted to hear. It was time Roarke knew how she really felt. Nothing mattered anymore, so she certainly couldn't make the situation any worse than it already was.

"You seem to forget, I have my memory back. I remember what our life together was like. You married a child and you were determined to keep me that way." Sara was pacing the room, the words pouring from her mouth of their own volition. She stopped in front of him, forcing him to meet her eyes. He was frozen, only his eyes followed her movements. They were hooded slits of blue steel, moving as she moved.

She started pacing again and moved away from Roarke. "You talk about games . . . games!" She threw her arms into the air in exasperation. "I played games to get a little attention from

177

you. It was the only way you ever took any notice of me at all. You know . . ." She stood in front of Roarke once more, shaking her finger in his face. "The only time you ever treated me like a woman was when we were in bed." She was in a red rage now, her fury seemed to have been uncapped like a volcano that had been latent for years then finally erupted from the internal pressure. All the years of pent-up frustration, hurt, and anger were pouring out and she couldn't stop. She was aware of Roarke only as the object of her tirade.

"You want to know what I was hysterical about? Well, I'll tell you. I was standing in here, wishing I could forget the past and my love for you." Sara laughed derisively. "Isn't this ironic? Can you imagine? For months I've driven myself nearly crazy trying to remember everything, and now that I have, I want to for-forget." Sara dropped her face into her hands and began crying bitterly.

Roarke moved across the room to her like a man still caught in a dream. Lovingly he took her into his arms, and when she tried to shake him off, he tightened his grip. "Sara, my darling Sara," he whispered into her ear. He stroked her hair and lifted her chin. His lips touched her brow, brushing across her forehead.

He coaxed her over to the bed and made her sit down beside him, his arm around her shoulders, holding her protectively close to him. He took a handkerchief out of his pocket and awkwardly dabbed her eyes.

Sara tried to shake off his arm and pulled the handkerchief from his grasp and wiped her own eyes. It would crush her to see his pity.

"Sara, look at me!" He forcibly turned her head and her eyes couldn't resist the compelling force of his order. Her breath caught in her throat and her heart quickened. It wasn't pity she saw in his eyes, it was love.

"Sara, I love you. I've always loved you. From the first time I saw you, I knew you would be the only woman I would ever

178

want." His voice thickened with emotion and his eyes glistened with unshed tears.

"Oh, Roarke, I can hardly believe this." She moved closer to him and tentatively touched a tear that escaped over his lashes. "Do you really love me?" she whispered.

"I have, all my life," Roarke answered, lowering his head toward her. Sara closed her eyes as his lips moved to touch hers. He pressed her back against the bed and gently stroked the sides of her face. She ran her hands restlessly over his back to reassure herself that he was there and not a dream.

"Can this be real? Is this true?" Sara asked hungrily, starved for reassurance.

"My darling, I've always loved you, always wanted you. And my real torture is knowing that no matter what happens between us, my love for you can't be destroyed." The tears that Sara had seen shimmering on his lashes dropped onto her chest and one trickled a warm path down between her breasts and lay shining in the hollow.

In awe Sara touched the moist droplet and looked at her fingertips then in breathless astonishment gently touched Roarke's cheek. Overwhelmed by his emotional reaction, she began to sob. "Roarke, there has never been anyone else, never. Please, love me, love me. You're all I want in life. I love you."

His kisses skimmed along her neck and his fingers fumbled a little at the buttons on her blouse. She sighed as the last button gave way and his lips fondled her breast. Entranced, Sara let a soft moan of pleasure escape her trembling lips. "How I love you, my darling, how I've longed to hold you close again, feel your body against mine and love you. I'm not complete without you. Even when I couldn't remember you, my body remembered your touch and my passion for you."

He lifted his fingers to her lips and whispered, "I love you, my darling." He cherished her unresisting lips once more with his. Their movements were intense and increased in tempo until they melted together in their old passion and their renewed love.

* * *

Sara was sitting up in bed propped against the pillows, her eyes sparkling and her cheeks still flushed from their shared ecstasy. Her lips were swollen from his kisses and she gingerly touched them, running her fingertips lightly across them, and she smiled to herself at different memories of their afternoon of delight.

She could hear Roarke in the kitchen whistling as he made coffee. The difference in him was unbelievable. No more guarded words, no mask over his face. He now had the expression that she loved—smiling happiness. His face held joy and contentment.

She wanted to get out of bed and look in the mirror to see if there was as dramatic a change in her as there was in him. He looked younger, years younger. A burden had been lifted from him, but it wasn't the burden she had worried about. Instead it was the burden of loving someone whom he thought didn't love him.

"Here we are, my love." His deep voice rumbled with delight.

Sara's heart welled with joy and she didn't know if she would be able to contain it. She threw back her head and laughed with the love and happiness that bubbled from inside her. Roarke stood beside the bed with only a towel wrapped around his waist, trying to balance the coffee cups on a tray, while trying to keep the towel from falling.

His muscles rippled as he placed the tray on the bed. The veins in his arms were like blue ropes winding their way up to his shoulders. He was magnificent! He sat down on the bed beside her with the tray between them. Sara leaned over and kissed him on the chest.

They sipped their coffee in silence, only their loving eyes holding a conversation. Then a shadow suddenly seemed to pass over Roarke's face and he moved the tray to the floor. "We have to talk, you know that, don't you?" He reached over and touched her cheek.

Sara looked at Roarke over the rim of her cup. She could only nod her head, because fear, like an icy blast of wind, gripped her insides.

"Don't look so frightened." He kissed her on the forehead, taking the cup from her hands as he gently pushed her back onto the pillows. He leaned over her, propped on one elbow. "You said a lot of things to me and about me that aren't true." He ran his finger down the side of her face and she nestled it between her shoulder and cheek.

Brushing her lips with his, he whispered, "I love you," as he shifted a little away from her so he could see her face and watch her reactions more closely. "I first saw you when you were seventeen years old. You were so beautiful. I fell in love with you then." He smiled at her tenderly; his eyes held a misty look of nostalgia. "I kept going to the house to see your grandmother on business, at least that's what I told myself. But the more I saw of you, the more I wanted to see you. I knew I was a lot older than you and that you were an innocent. Yet every time I was near you, I wanted to take you into my arms and hold you. So I decided to go to London to get away from you for a while, thinking if I didn't see so much of you or know you were close, I could maybe fall in love with someone else. But it didn't work. I couldn't forget you. Then I received the letter from your grandmother telling me she was dying and begging me to take care of you after she was gone." He caressed her face with his hand.

"I married you because I loved you, not because I felt responsible for you. I know now that I treated you wrongly, I didn't treat you like a wife. I was afraid to treat you like a woman. I knew you had a crush on me, but I wondered if it was real love. I wanted to give you time to learn to love me."

Sara put her fingers over his lips. "We were both wrong, Roarke, I did so many childish things, stupid things. Even my jealousy was immature. When I saw that file folder in your office the day I told you I was leaving you, I just knew you didn't love me, that I was nothing more than an obligation and a responsibility that a promise to an old lady trapped you into honoring. I

181

convinced myself you had just wanted the business and I was the means to your keeping it. When you walked into the office that day with Suzanne and she was so smug, I was totally convinced my thinking was correct."

"Damn it, Sara, I told you then that you were behaving irrationally!" he sat up abruptly. "That letter from your grandmother had nothing to do with my decision to marry you." Roarke shook his head in remembered disgust. "That damned file folder. Honey, I kept legal documents like your power of attorney and other important papers in there. The letters from your grandmother were in it because I felt you might want them someday. If only you would have believed me when I told you I loved you instead of running out of my office in a damned flaming rage." His brows lowered over eyes reflecting a little of the hurt and bitterness still remembered from that day.

"No, Roarke," Sara murmured as she reached out and stroked his arm. "I wasn't ready to believe you then. It took the two years of us being apart for me to start appreciating what we had and to realize what I had lost. And everywhere I went I saw you with Suzanne and thought you loved her. That stopped me cold every time I weakened and thought of trying to talk with you."

He gathered her into his arms and held her close. "Suzanne is another story, darling. Suzanne ."

"Why did you let her pretend to be my friend?" Sara interrupted. "Why did you let her try to fool me? Why didn't you stop her?"

"I felt if I made an issue of it then you'd only think I was trying to keep you isolated. Plus, I was afraid, Sara. Afraid that if I told you all about Suzanne, you'd remember, remember everything!" He released her from his arms and sat on the edge of the bed.

Sara knelt at his back, embracing him from behind, holding him close. "Are you . . . are you and Suzanne . . . lovers?" Sara whispered, frightened by what his answer might be. What if he said yes? Could she cope with that knowledge, and was her love strong enough to help her to forgive him and forget it?

He turned his face away from her but not quickly enough so that she didn't see the look of shame and anguish flush over it. Her heart stopped. She had her answer! Her arms went limp for a fraction of a second, then, bowing her head, she placed her forehead on the smooth skin of his back and lightly touched the satin firmness with her lips. No matter what he said, she knew and now had to live forever knowing for certain that somehow, through hunger, need, or whatever the reason, for a small part of her life with Roarke, she had shared him.

Her hands ran over his muscular chest, her fingertips catching themselves and entangling in the curls that covered it. Tears gathered on her lashes as she murmured against his back, her breath making the skin under her cheek feel hot, "Don't answer that, darling. I don't want to hear the answer. It doesn't matter now."

Roarke twisted his body in her arms, but she kept her face firmly against his back, her hands clutching him to keep him from seeing her face. She didn't want him to know that she knew. "Sara . . ." Roarke gasped, "I—"

"Roarke," Sara whispered low and huskily, "there's only one thing I need to hear about her from you. I thought you wanted to marry her. She told me that you were going to divorce me and marry her and I believed her. She had keys to this apartment and told me she was living here after she had moved out of our house. Of course, once I remembered everything, I realized she was lying, but how did she get the keys? Were you going to divorce me?"

Roarke turned his head to glance at her over his shoulder. "She lied . . . lied about everything, Sara. When I got home the other day and Martha said you were here at the apartment, I called and called, but you didn't answer the phone. I called Suzanne, since she lives near here and asked her to go to the office and get the key and check to see if you were here. That's how she got the key. As for living in our house—that's a damnable lie!" He grasped her hand and caressed it with his lips. "I couldn't have divorced you! When you told me yesterday that you wanted a divorce, I almost broke apart. After I left here, I drove for hours and hours just thinking about us and trying to figure out a way to convince you that I loved you and didn't want to lose you. That's why I called at four this morning. I had just gotten home and received the message that you called."

He turned to look at her again. "Darling, when I got the call that you had been seriously injured and I was to get to the hospital immediately, I almost died. When Ted told me there was some doubt that you would survive the accident, I wanted to die along with you."

Sara shivered and hugged him close and kissed his nape. He put his hands over hers that she had entwined around his chest and held them tighter to his body.

"Your memory loss seemed to be a gift from heaven," he continued in a low voice. "I thought we could start our lives over with a clean slate. I was determined to go slowly and not pressure you. I wanted to give you time to know me again and hopefully learn to love me. I wanted to forget the hurtful things from the past also. I felt you were almost lucky not to be able to remember."

Sara sighed. "I've done a lot of things these past two years that make me ashamed when I think of them. I don't have any excuse except that I loved you and didn't know how to tell you or how to make you love me. I used other men to make you jealous."

Sara leaned her head against his back and tightened her arms around him, the firm flesh of his back warm against her bare breasts and her cheek. "I never meant to hurt you, but I couldn't understand the way you treated me."

"We have a lot of making up to do to each other, Sara. I know I treated you horribly most of the time you were ill. I don't have an excuse either, except that I looked on your memory loss as our last chance to start over and undo all the wrongs of the past.

"When you would have a flashback, I would panic, thinking your memory was returning and I'd lose you again. I just couldn't cope with the idea of you remembering even the smallest detail. I reacted badly, I know. Instead of being mature and facing the probable return of your memory, I mentally denied it would happen. Instead of helping you, I was so afraid, I closed you off. Built up the wall you felt.

"The miracle seemed to be that with your memory loss, you had become the woman I always dreamed you would be. I was afraid that if you remembered everything, you'd be the immature child again." He let go of her hands that held his chest and ran his fingers through his hair. Turning around, he took her face between his hands. The look in his eyes made Sara's heart ache.

"But the worst was when I came here to the apartment to take you back home and I realized you had run away. I called everyone I could think of, including Ted. When he said he hadn't seen you or heard from you, we decided we'd better start searching." Roarke shuddered. "When I think of you wandering around this city all night, not knowing where you were . . ."

Sara wrapped her body protectively around him again. "I ran away because I couldn't face you, Roarke. I loved you so much and Suzanne had led me to believe you two were living together. It just reinforced my belief that you thought of me as your unwanted burden. I couldn't stay here and see the two of you together, see your love for each other. I had to get away. I didn't stop to think about where I was going or what I was going to do. I couldn't remember myself as the person you seemed to despise so much and I couldn't understand how I could be what I am now, with the feelings I have, and also be the person you remembered so bitterly. Every time a piece of the past was revealed, I couldn't believe I was so shallow and mean. The only thing I knew was that I loved you and I couldn't stand to live with your anger or your pity any longer." Sara bowed her head as the memory of that frightening night alone in the city flashed through her mind.

Roarke kissed the top of her head and put two fingers under her chin, lifting it so her eyes would meet his. "We've done a lot of foolish things, my love. We've hurt each other and, in the end, nearly destroyed each other. Now we have our new start, Sara. The new beginning we've both been praying for."

"Yes, we do," Sara smiled into his eyes.

"I need you, I want you. I don't want to exist without you," he said huskily, taking her in his arms.

"And I don't want to live without you." Sara snuggled against him. "I'm glad it's over, it's finally over. Our past, present, and future have at last all fallen into place." She raised her lips to meet his as his arms closed around her, enveloping her in his warmth. Slowly, sensuously, their bodies moved together, building a passion that had existed in their past and bound them together forever.

A love forged by destiny—
A passion born of flame

FLAMES
OF
DESIRE

by Vanessa Royall

Selena MacPherson, a proud princess of ancient
Scotland, had never met a man who did not desire
her. From the moment she met Royce Campbell at
an Edinburgh ball, Selena knew the burning
ecstasy that was to seal her fate through all eternity.
She sought him on the high seas, in India, and
finally in a young America raging in the
birth-throes of freedom, where destiny was bound
to fulfill its promise. . . .

A DELL BOOK $2.95

Come Faith, Come Fire

Vanessa Royall

Proud as her aristocratic upbringing, bold as the ancient gypsy blood that ran in her veins, the beautiful golden-haired Maria saw her family burned at the stake and watched her young love, forced into the priesthood. Desperate and bound by a forbidden love, Maria defies the Grand Inquisitor himself and flees across Spain to a burning love that was destined to be free!

A Dell Book $2.95 (12173-6)